# Horrid Mysteries.

## A STORY.

### FROM THE GERMAN OF THE MARQUIS OF GROSSE.

### BY P. WILL.

IN FOUR VOLUMES.

### VOL. III.

LONDON:

PRINTED FOR *WILLIAM LANE, AT THE*
Minerva-Press,

LEADENHALL-STREET.

M DCC XCVI.

# THE
# HORRID MYSTERIES.

## CHAPTER I.

### *Extract from Elmira's Papers.*

I AWOKE, at length, from that long fwoon, and found myfelf ftretched out in a coffin. Some more of the receptacles of the wrecks of mortality ftood near me, and the odour of corruption was the firft thing that affected my fenfes. The fpacious and lofty vault was fparingly lighted by the faint glimmer of a fingle lamp, that was fufpended to the ceiling. Its dying flame plainly told me where I was. What mortal can conceive a juft idea of the fenfations produced by the firft breaking from fleep under fuch circumftances; and who could be able to recal only a fingle fentiment of thofe that crowded on

VOL. III.          B          my

my mind, if he ever was fo unfortunate
to have experienced what I did? I did not
know what I fhould do in that dreadful
fituation; whether I fhould call for affiftance, or patiently await the event. The
lamp was a certain proof that I was in a
place not entirely deferted by human
beings; and I felt no other painful fenfation, but a great weaknefs, and relaxation
of my bodily and mental faculties. Yet
I was not fuffered to remain long in a ftate
of confultation with myfelf; the found of
different voices vibrating in my ears from
a paffage whofe entrance the dying glimmer of the lamp enabled me to defcry. I
even could diftinguifh the expreffions and
the fubjeĉt of their difcourfe. Some de-
claimed againft Carlos's inhuman barba-
rity, and fome cenfured me for my imprudence; but one perfon defended me,
finding it very natural that a weak, love-
fick, and inexperienced girl fhould have
been taken in by an artful and experienced
villain. The talkers, having carefully
ftopt

ſtopt a while at the entrance, came, at
length, nearer, and appeared in the vault,
exhibiting a large proceſſion of compaſ-
ſionate faces of either ſex. Some carried
torches, ſome phials and glaſſes, and ſome
garments and linen. The light, that
now illuminated my horrid reſidence, en-
abling me to look around, I beheld myſelf enfolded in a cloud, and different
veſſels ſtanding by my ſide.

"Loud rejoicings re-echoed through
the vault when my viſitors ſaw me ſitting
in the coffin; and they ran towards me to
complete my reſuſcitation, carrying me
out of the damp cavern to a lofty apartment, where I was put into a well aired
bed. Decency bade my deliverers to retire, and only two females ſtaid with me,
to aſſiſt me in changing my dreſs, while I
gradually was re-animated with a pleaſing
warmth, and recovered the full power of
recollection.

"When they ſaw that I had entirely recovered my faculties, they congratulated
me

me on my prefervation, praifing God for having made them inftrumental in my reftoration to life.

" Thank God, Countefs," one of them began, " that you have been refcued from the cruel hands of that barbarian, and are now in the company of more humane beings!"

" From what cruel hands?" I replied, with aftonifhment.

" From thofe of your pretended lover, the Marquis Carlos of G******."

" Be filent, vile reptile," I exclaimed, " and dare not to afperfe the name of a man whom I adore!"

" Don't put yourfelf into a paffion, my Lady," fhe replied coolly: " You will be of our opinion before many days are elapfed. We are members of a fociety whofe fole bufinefs it is to make the fufferer forget his forrows, and to reftore the unhappy to happinefs. Indeed, Countefs, we flattered ourfelves to deferve, at leaft, your gratitude."

" What

" What could I have replied to the declaration of that woman in my fituation?
I was filent; and having taken a firm refolution to conceal all my ideas, I diſſembled to rely implicitly on the candour of
my pretended deliverers. It was but too
evident in whoſe power I was; and what I
had heard of that fociety on my wedding-
day forced itſelf with additional ſtrength on
my recollection. Though I could not
unfold the real purport of that incident,
yet it was fufficient to afcertain to me the
truth of my fufpicions. If, therefore, it
was poſſible to extricate myſelf from their
fnares, no other expedient was left than to
pay them in their own coin, and to attempt to outwit them by a diſſimulation
fuperior to theirs. I began, therefore, to
pretend being more fufceptible of the
ideas which they endeavoured to inſtil into
my mind, and returned gradually from
my gloomy reveries. I was, indeed, partial to folitude; however, it appeared to
them to be favourable to their fecret de-

B 3                     figns

figns upon me; and the more the refult of my contemplations feemed to make me uneafy, the lefs miftruft againft their fecret endeavours to encreafe thofe diftreffing doubts did I difplay. I fubmitted, with an unaffected reluctance, more and more, to their attempts at diverting my mind, and to their exertions to reftore me to happinefs, as they pretended, and to return me to my family with an eafier heart. A cheerful gaiety, which I kept in proper bounds, and ftrove to render as natural as poffible, by an impofing varnifh of truth, confirmed them in their belief of having gained upon my credulity; and I began to hope that I fhould find a favourable moment to give them the flip. I was not anxious to know the external circumftances of the confederates, thinking myfelf fufficiently happy if I could but efcape their baneful breath.

"Mean time a number of fine ladies and gentlemen gathered around me. I was invited to accompany them on a nocturnal

turnal excursion to a neighbouring castle,
where I learnt, the next morning, that it
was to be my future residence. The situa-
tion was, indeed, beautiful; the garden
extensive and elegant; walking was, therefore, my chief occupation and amuse-
ment. Although I was never without
company, or at least without such attendants as observed me from a distance, and
the happy period of my elopement was
probably not very near, yet I cheered myself up by numberless plans of accelerating it secretly.

" My keepers studied to amuse me by
numberless little diversions. Rural feasts,
the charm of selected parties; beautiful, winning females, and young, amiable men, were to accomplish, with the
smiling assistance of the graces, during a
constant round of pleasures, what had
been devised and begun under circumstances of the most serious and awful complexion. Every one breathed a general
and delicate desire of pleasing me, and of

anticipating

anticipating my wifhes before they had
time to ripen to maturity; and I cannot
but confefs, that they feveral times accomplifhed their defigns as perfectly as they
could wifh.   I returned involuntarily their
kindnefs, as if enchanted.   They fucceeded to make me more unreferved; and
if not the few hours, in which I was not
in their company, had weakened the im-
preffions of the reft, I fhould fcarcely have
been able to avoid an intoxication which
would have ruined me for ever.

   " Amongft the young men by whom I
was furrounded, one diftinguifhed himfelf particularly.   He was of a moft
beautiful form, animated with a very dangerous fire, of polifhed manners, and an
infinuating difpofition, which rendered
him pliable to all my wifhes.   He feemed
to claim my favour in a more particular
manner than the reft, depended entirely
upon my looks, and was happy or unhappy as my humour changed.   Never have
the wiles of the moft cunning feduction
                              been

been applied in a more artful manner; all circumftances were in his favour: whatever the reft of the company faid, fupported and advanced his fuperiority; and being, in the fequel, convinced of the purity of his paffion, by his indefatigable exertions to pleafe me, I could not have avoided being caught in the fnare at Iaft, if not a trifling accident had rectified my opinion of him, and reftored me to myfelf and to my plans.

" He had a little French dog; and I grew fo foolifhly fond of the animal, that I frequently hinted to him, it would give me the greateft pleafure if he would make me a prefent of it; yet he feemed not to be inclined to part with his little favourite. At length he promifed me, one afternoon, to let me have it in the evening. I was walking fometime before the affembly hour in the bofcage, and paffing the entrance of a bower, faw him in it, feated on a bench, and occupied with his favourite, and concealed myfelf behind a

B 5 : thick

thick hazel-bufh.   He tied a ribband
round the neck of his little darling, and
having finifhed the tafk, he could not refrain from kiffing him, and uttering the
words, " Poor Thonon! we muft part:
however, thou wilt always be dearer to me
than what thou art to purchafe for me."

" Thefe words wounded my heart like
a dagger; and my whole fituation lay, at
once, undifguifed before my eyes.   I was
ready to faint; and could fcarcely refrain
from rufhing forth, and letting him fee
an Elmira entirely different from that he
had known till then.   Yet rage and pain
fortunately ftifled my tears and fighs, and
I arrived at my apartment without being
feen by him.

" As foon as I had recovered my recollection, I faw plainly how neceffary it was
not to give up the part I had begun to act.
I prevailed upon myfelf, after a hard
ftruggle, to affume again the femblance
of cheerfulnefs, and an air of tranquil refignation.   The dog was prefented to me,
                                    and

and received with an impofing pleafure: the donor expected, and demanded, at length, a reward for the facrifice he had made to me; but being cautioned by what I had overheard, I found it pretty eafy to evade his violent careffes and tender menaces.

 "Thus fome weeks more elapfed, and I could ftill not find out proper means of effecting my efcape. The danger of a longer ftay grew every day more preffing. I knew, however, neither the diftrict in which the caftle was fituated, nor the neighbourhood, and was carefully guarded. At length I attempted, with a very fmall probability of fuccefs, what I, perhaps, under more favourable circumftances, never had dared to rifk. At a feaft, which was given on my account, and on which all eyes were directed at me, I got fuddenly from my throne, on which I was to receive an approaching proceffion, upon a walnut-tree, and fortunately concealed
myfelf.

myself between the thick branches till night promised to favour my flight!

" I defcended from my afylum as foon as it was dark. A foot-path led me to a neighbouring village; and the darknefs of night protected me on my retreat. Being animated with a more than common courage, I ventured to enter a cottage, exchanged my garments for a rural drefs, dyed my face, and begged my way through the provinces of Spain and France to this peaceful fpot. I loft, indeed, on my journey, a part of the jewels with which they had decorated me; yet I faved a fufficient quantity to purchafe this little folitude, and to commence a little farm, which promifed to afford me a frugal fupport for the remainder of my life?"

## CHAPTER II.

" THE above chapter, dearest Count, is a faithful, but brief, extract from that part of Elmira's hiftory of which

which I was ignorant till then. You fee how fingular the turn of her and of my fate was directed by a higher Power. If ever I had been capable to doubt that Providence guides the fate of man, the reflections which her account produced, would certainly have convinced me of the eternal truth, that a benevolent Being watches over our life and happinefs, and produces light out of darknefs.

"Give me now leave to inform you of the remainder of my adventures, which I fhall be able to conclude in a few words. Clara was in love with the fon of a neighbouring farmer; but being poor, and the father of her lover a rich man, the latter would not confent to a union between his fon and her. Being averfe to fell or to abalienate any thing my fainted Elmira had poffeffed, I gave her the confiderable produce of my little eftate as a dowry, faw the young couple married, and went through Swifferland and Germany to G******,

G******, where I had the happiness to make your acquaintance.

" You know my history from that day: suffice it, therefore, to tell you briefly, that while you was fighting the battles of your country against Great Britain, I went to B******, to commence a private, but, nevertheless, not inactive life, and to en- joy those pleasures I was accustomed to. I shall not tire your patience with an account of the little adventures, and the unimpor- tant events, of that period in which I was constantly surrounded by members of secret societies, and enthusiasts of all forts, got possession of their secrets, and ob- served that they were far inferior to what I already knew, or that they were partly connected with the confederacy in Spain."

. I shall here, at last, take up again the thread of those events I have mentioned in the middle of my adventures, which I have wrote down for the Count. The reader will recollect that a man (James) settled in our neighbourhood, who, as I apprehended,

apprehended, was nearly connected with
me. His appearance threatened me with
new misfortunes; and he feemed to intend
opening a new way of influence on me
through the heart of the Count. However, that ominous apparition paffed
quickly over. He had, indeed, pur-
chafed a country feat in the neighbourhood; but difappeared after a few days.
I was told that he was going to B*******
on matrimonial affairs, and my apprehenfions vanifhed. That incident left, however, fome impreffion on my mind; and
many plans, particularly that of returning
to my native country, were thereby obliterated from my foul. I comprehended
many a myfterious phenomenon more
clearly, and could, in fome degree, account for Amanuel's apparitions, the
frequent repetition of which now appeared
to me to be a great imprudence of the
unknown confederates. They probably
intended to frighten me, by letting me
fee that I was furrounded every where by
their

their fecret agents: however, the myftic
appearance of Amanuel's prefence, which
had affected my fenfes fo powerfully, loft
its awfulnefs entirely through that over-
fight.  I was no ftranger to the artifices
wrought through natural magic; and alfo
not ignorant what a powerful influence a
heated, overflowing, and tranfported imagination produces on our fenfes.  The
whole now appeared to me a mere fcare-
crow for children.  The myftic farce was
continued too long, and afterwards betrayed the whole confederacy.  The myfterious veil was removed from that memorable
moment, and my imagination being rectified by cool reflection, the miferable
artifices of the confederates rather filled
me with contempt than with awe. James's
apparition in my neighbourhood opened
my eyes; and my mind, being now libe-
rated from the thraldom of a deluded
imagination, firmly begins a new, decided
career.

The

The Count was very much grieved at the fudden departure of the dear ftranger, as he ufed to call him. I was already, in the beginning, ftrongly tempted to predict it; but cannot conceive what prevented me from doing fo; and my friend was, foon after that incident, a fecond time obliged, by his affairs, to leave me, before I could conclude my hiftory, and elucidate many myfterious events to him; for the various occupations in which I was engaged did not allow me, as I already have informed the reader, more leifure hours for the continuation of my memoirs than I could fpare from the time of nocturnal reft.

My friend remained a long time abfent, being detained by the unaccountable intricacy of his affairs. It really feemed as if they intended to exhauft his patience by juridical chicanes and petty artifices, to make him wafte his precious time in the moft ufelefs manner. I very feldom received letters from him, and he always
concluded

concluded them by informing me that he should not return so soon. Being convinced that I was completely acquainted with his ideas, he did not trouble himself about the management of his estates, which was an additional motive for me to be the more careful. There never was a period in my whole life, in which I knew so well to fill up every moment with such exactness; every one of them, from morning till night, being counted and designed for some employment. These tedious occupations did not at first please me much on account of their tiresome sameness; however, after a few weeks reluctant exertion, they grew so easy, and at last so amusing to me, that I could not disuse myself therefrom. I now exercised more authority over the Count's people than he ever did himself, because he had not acquired that knowledge of the inferior classes which I possessed: I conversed with every one, listened to every proposal of theirs, and frequently improved my
own

own plans by comparing and uniting their
ideas with mine. I was all the day long
on horfeback, or running from one part
of the eftate to the other, to give direc-
tions to the workmen. I never indulged
myfelf with reading before all the labourers had finifhed their daily tafk, and
my accounts were fettled; and after fupper, which received an additional relifh
from the fatigues of the day, I continued
my memoirs till it was time to go to reft,
when I went to bed highly fatisfied with
myfelf. The writing down of my memoirs was, from that time, continued with
fo much affiduity, that the manufcript
was finifhed in lefs than a month after the
Count's departure. I afterwards correded
it in many places, and gave it him on his
return.

I was always very fond of gardening;
and although my friend had an excellent
tafte in arranging the whole, yet he had
too little patience to dedicate much time
to a proper furvey and regulation of the
particulars.

particulars. I began, therefore, to revife
his excellent plans, and to polifh them
more carefully than he had taken the trouble to do, and altered fome parts of his
garden accordingly. Some old buildings
and pleafure houfes were facrificed to my
impatient induftry. A pavilion, which
was fituated in a corner of the park, and
vifited by no one who valued his life, was
one of the chief objects that had excited
my diflike. It was entirely concealed by
bufhes and trees, and feemed to have been
defigned by nature for folitude, which determined me to have it pulled down, and
to build in its place a little hermitage,
with a few fmall apartments; flattering
myfelf with the fweet hope of being able
to inhabit them the fubfequent fummer.
I formed that idea and the plan for the
new building in one night; went early in
the morning into the garden, took fome
workmen with me, who were cleaning a
bafon, ordering them to provide themfelves with the neceffary implements, and
                              conducted

conducted them to the pavilion, with the
inftruction to pull the old neft inftantly
down. My orders were put into execution
with the greateft alacrity. A part of one
of the fide-walls fell down of itfelf; and
a large ftone, which feemed to fupport the
reft, being removed, we beheld the entrance of a narrow fubterraneous paffage.
We ftared at each other, ·feized with aftoniſhment; and I aſked one of the workmen whether he could ftrike fire? He af-
firmed it; and fome of his fellow labourers
tore fome dry branches from a fir-tree,
which, being lighted, the whole train followed me laughing into the cavern, ex-
pecting to find a great treafure, and to
have fome fhare of it. We defcended,
therefore, cheerfully; and I cannot deny
that I alfo hoped to find fomething of
value, though of a different nature from
what they imagined. The fcene which
once took place between myfelf and the
Count in that very garden, the fmall diftance of the famous turf-feat from the
- pavilion,

pavilion, the communication of thefe two places through an almoft impenetrable bofcage, and the favourable concealment of the fpot, feemed to promife me fome important difcovery, which was the rea-fon of my being more apprehenfive than the reft of my fellow adventurers. How-ever, the confideration of my being at-tended by feven ftout Germans, armed with their working tools, and of a brave appearance, foon infpired me with cou-rage. I entered the avenue laughing, though with a beating heart, and called to the reft to keep clofe to my heels. I left one at the avenue, to guard us againft all external attacks; and to alarm the fervants at the caftle, if we fhould not return within the courfe of an hour. Having defcended fome part of our way almoft perpendicularly, the paffage grew fo fmall, that we found it very difficult to proceed. I conftantly held the torch before me, ex-amining the ground carefully, left we fhould be caught in a dangerous fnare.

Yet,

Yet, the paffage foon grew wider, the way more even; and we had not proceeded a minute, when we came, into a vaulted cave, which apparently formerly was a cellar. We difcovered, in the back part, a fecond receptacle, furnifhed with a table and chairs, that were pretty new. On examining the table, I found that a piece had recently been cut out of it; and it appeared to me that fome perfon had attempted to obliterate a character which feemed to have been cut into the wood. After a more minute infpection, I difcovered fome traces of an E.

I could not guefs, at firft, what that letter could mean, but recollected, at laft, that the Count had the fingular cuftom to delineate frequently fuch an E in the fand, or to cut it into the bark of trees; and I ere now fufpected that letter to be the firft character of the name of a former miftrefs. I difcovered nothing elfe befides this; neither a new avenue, nor a continuation of the vault. I had ordered all

4

my

my attendants to fearch every corner:
however, we found no farther trace of a
human inhabitation; yet, when I left the
vault, to afcend the paffage again, one of
them exclaimed, that he had found fome
papers. I ordered him to give them to
me, and unfolded them. All of them
were blank, except the fourth, on which
fomething was written, and I was ftruck
with aftonifhment when I read, "*Countefs
Elmira is cautioned againft the young Marquis Carlos of G****** who means to impofe
upon her.*" I did not know whether I
could truft my eyes; yet it was undoubtedly the fame paper. Seeing, however,
that my attendants were aftonifhed to fee
me ftart back, I added coolly, after a few
moments confideration, " The D——l
may make that out without the other
half."

So faying, I threw the whole parcel into
the fame corner in which it had been
found. Thus terminated that fingular
expedition. I left the paffage with an eafy
heart;

heart; but my conductors hung their heads, becaufe they had not found the expected treafures. In order to confole them for their difappointment, I gave every one a dollar, under the condition to mention nothing of our adventure to the Count's fervants. I could eafily forefee that this would be the fureft means of having it circulated in the caftle, and determined to watch whether I could gather nothing from the behaviour of the fervants, all of whom I fufpected very much. However, the whole affair became a fubject of general merriment: every one was impatient to fee the fubterraneous vault; and the vifits of the curious to the cellar became foon fo numerous, that I ordered the paffage to be fhut up, becaufe it was now the general rendezvous of the fervants. Thus terminated that adventure. The new pavilion was finifhed in a fhort time, and furnifhed, and I had the pleafure of breakfafting there before the Count returned. He arrived at length, fatigued

VOL. III.       C       by

by the incidents and the labours which had retarded his return so long. His affairs were, indeed, settled, and his law-suit was gained: however, the expences amounted to more than he had saved; and he had, besides, reason to regret the time he had wasted in that disagreeable affair. Yet he thought himself rewarded for his troubles, in some degree, by several discoveries he had accidentally made, and which he communicated to me without reserve as soon as he had read my memoirs.

"Let us act just, dear Carlos," he said, "notwithstanding those villainous artifices. We are not bound to keep promises which have been forced from us by cruelties: it would, however, be to no purpose to inform you of the history of those days when I suddenly left you. You have discovered the mysteries of the cavern: it seems to be forsaken already for some time, and I have made a solemn promise to be silent. What is, at present, of

more

more importance to me, is to find out the perfons that ftill are very active in our neighbourhood, that have confounded my law-fuit, and, as I have reafon to apprehend, will ruin us fooner or later. Marquis, are you my friend?" Here he ftretched out his hand. I fhook it warmly, and replied, "Yes, I am your fincere, your faithful friend."

"Will you ever preferve me your affection?" "By Heaven! for ever!" "Then come to my heart, my brother, and receive from me the fame vow. I fwear to be inviolably your friend; and may I be left without comfort in my dying hour, if ever I forget this promife only for a fingle moment. May Heaven preferve me your friendfhip; this is all that I wifh."

"Lewis, I follow you whitherfoever you go, in fpite of all difafters that may befall you."

"Well, then, let us boldly meet thofe daring villains that intrude upon our fate;

C 2                                    let

let us fave the laft half of life; let us facrifice a few years more, and without
mercy attack them in the centre of their
myftic abode."

" Here is my hand. I follow you."

" Let us go to Paris, affemble our
friends around us, and then penetrate into
Spain. How willingly would I facrifice
the greater part of my fortune in that attempt, if I could purchafe peace and
tranquillity."

## CHAPTER III.

WE now exerted ourfelves jointly to
fettle the Count's affairs as well as
it was poffible. Before fix months were
elapfed, we accomplifhed our purpofe,
and foon after arrived at the capital of
France.

We were obliged to mix with the great
world, in order to make difcoveries, and
to obtain all kinds of affiftance in the execution of our plans. The Count fpared
nothing

nothing to do credit to his rank and title, and to introduce himfelf with *eclat*. His equipage was one of the moft fplendid at Paris; his fervants' liveries were in the higheft tafte; his drefs was felected with elegance; and before many weeks were elapfed, we were introduced in the beft circles of the town, and in fome received with cordiality.

The amufements of that capital are too well known to require a minute defcrip-tion. The play, dancing, parties of plea-fure, and particularly the charm of the fine arts, never mifs their aim. The Count was not much attracted by them. My character, on the contrary, impels me forcibly to feek that fort of amufement. We mixed, therefore, with the gay circles, and enjoyed the pleafures of Paris, but without being much diverted. We made new connexions, and continued the old ones, without facrificing much to them; and fpared every day at leaft a few hours

for

for more important converfations in our clofet.

It was very favourable to our purpofe, that many of my former acquaintances and friends gradually gathered around us. Don Bernhard and Count S******i were the firft, and more ·ftrongly captivated with our plans than I had left them. They were furprifed to the higheft degree at Count S******'s adventures, and impatient to have thofe myfterious incidents elucidated. The fufferings and experiences of fome years had ripened our characters, and rendered them more harmonious; and we found, in the mutual exchange of our ideas, comforts, pleafures, and profpects which none of us had expected.

Our method of proceeding was alfo altered very much through the exifting circumftances. Having divefted ourfelves of our former timidity, we made no fecret of our plans, but fpoke of them wherever we met; and while we thus gained many
friends

friends and fharers in our enterprize, we alfo obtained gradually more refources, and perhaps, defeated thereby many fecret machinations of the confederates.

Yet all thefe favourable circumftances did not, at bottom, bring us much nearer to the mark; for all our power confifted, as yet, in nothing elfe than in firmnefs, and in a calculated oppofition againft probable future events. We had not fixed upon a plan of attack, but left the regulation of our proceedings to the direction of circumftances; yet nothing happened that could have guided us. The Count was inclined to return to Spain; and I would have faithfully followed him, if it had not been for Don Bernhard, and our affociated friends, without whofe affiftance we could not expect to fucceed in our undertaking, which, to confefs the truth, promifed very little, as the centre of the confederacy could eafily be fhifted; and we had already been convinced that it could exift any where. Thus our prepa-

C 4

rations

rations were rendered ineffective by the confederates, while they took care to give us no opportunity of applying vigorous meafures. We began, by degrees, to grow negligent, becaufe no occafion occurred that could have given energy to our defigns. Trifling amufements enervated our defire for great and important deeds; and the female world left us little time to meditate on ferious occupations. A conftant round of diverfions unbraced our minds; and we foon looked upon our plans, which formerly had engaged our whole attention, as an object of exercifing our wit. At laft an incident happened which feemed to make us forget them entirely. A fatal love affair occafioned a difference between myfelf and the Count; deprived me, for a long time, of his affection and confidence, before I could prevail upon myfelf to make fome facrifice to him; and, furprifing us unawares, almoft terminated our inveftigations by an ill-fated jealoufy. Chance only re-united

us,

us, and removed the veil of myfteriouf-
nefs from our eyes.

Caroline de B****** was of an ancient
and noble family in Picardy. She was
not rich; however, her fortune was fufficient to afford her a good education, and
to render her no defpicable party. She
was not handfome; but her complexion
was frefh, her fhape elegant, and her deportment natural and winning. She poffeffed an unaffected gaiety, which graced
all her movements, and gave them diver-
fity and novity. She neither poffeffed a
ftriking wit, nor an uncommon underftanding: however, her fallies were always
pleafing; and her modefty, good-nature,
and evennefs of temper, fpoke highly in
her favour. As for her character, I might
well fay, fhe had none; it was, at leaft,
impoffible to difcern it; for fhe accommodated herfelf with fo much eafe and fimplicity to the individual difpofition of
thofe with whom fhe converfed, and
adapted herfelf in fo natural a manner to

C 5                              the

the humours of thofe with whom fhe was
connected, that every one imagined to fee
in her his own picture.   As for her heart,
I may truly fay that it was pure and
noble.

It was, indeed, very unfortunate for us
that we did not get fooner acquainted with
that amiable being.  If we had feen her
on our introduction into our focial circle,
the impreffion fhe would have made upon
us, would, perhaps, not have been fo
ftrong, or foon have been obliterated by
other charming objects.  But now we
were tired by too much art; and our hearts
being over-fatigued by the intricate mazes
of the moft confummate female coquetry,
were in want of a place of reft in the lap
of fimple nature.

Caroline charmed us at firft fight.  We
got acquainted with her at an evening affembly which we frequented almoft every
day to play at cards.  Caroline had already,
fometime before our arrival, accompanied
fome friends into the country; and being
a conftant

a conftant member of the cheerful circle where we met her, her return occafioned fome confufion in the arrangement of the gaming-party. As foon as fhe perceived this, fhe declared that fhe would not play with us, but was determined to be received again into the party to which fhe belonged before fhe went into the country. This whim threw the whole company into a new confufion. Thofe with whom fhe defired to affociate again, were already ufed to their new companions, and did not fhew the leaft inclination to quit them; and their ladies were not lefs difinclined to be abandoned by their partners on Caroline's account. The general commotion to which this gave rife terminated at laft in a loud laughter, which covered the face of the poor girl with a high crimfon colour, and fhe declared that fhe would not play at all. Tranquillity and order were foon reftored, and I feated myfelf by her fide on the fofa; not ill pleafed with the termination of that ridiculous affair.

C 6 However,

However, the Count's mind was far from being easy. It is almost impossible to brook such an incident with indifference with an irritability like his, which was unimpaired by misfortunes. Anger boiled in his heart, and he only wanted an opportunity of giving vent to it. A fire, whose nature I was no stranger to, flushed in his eye, and seemed to search an object. I ridiculed his agitation, and begged him to be easy: however, he replied; "Fye upon you, Carlos; how can you be so torpid?" "He then fixed his eyes upon a German officer, who played at some distance from us, and continued to smile at our disaster. "Don't you comprehend," he resumed, "that all this is pre-concerted?"

He was, perhaps, not much mistaken, if he suspected the German officer, who called himself Baron de H******, to have acted in this affair with some malicious heat, and with design. Yet he was not a man that could submit to be scoffed at

without

without chaftifing the offender. He knew the Baron already at Gibraltar, where he had fought with him againſt the Britons, and, by a ſtrange accident, was his rival in the love of a Spaniſh lady. This had already incenſed him againſt the Baron; and an affair of a later date, which I am going to relate, made him his implacable enemy.

The Count kept an actreſs of the royal opera, a charming girl, of uncommon wit, and a great knowledge of man; an excellent companion, but not very famous for her fidelity. Although he was not over fond of her, keeping her rather for faſhion's ſake than from inclination, yet he looked upon her favours as goods which he had bought, and which no one could intrude upon without violating his property. His vanity contributed to render his ambition ſtill more tender with regard to that point; and there was a period when his mind was entirely occupied with plans of ſecuring the fidelity of his Amaſia

againſt

againſt all temptations which might be thrown into her way. But how was it poſſible he could have interrupted all the connections of a vain, voluptuous, and covetous girl, who had made it the ſtudy of her life to infnare men, and to jilt them, in her fetters? In ſhort, he had fuf-ficient reaſon for being jealous, and par-ticularly of his ſworn rival, Baron de H******.

An odd incident ſerved to blow up that dormant fire into a blazing flame. He went one evening over the Pont Neuf to pay her a viſit; and intending to furprife her unexpectedly, to be certain of her in-fidelity, he had put on a blue coat, and taken only one ſervant with him. On coming to the middle of the bridge, he was at once furrounded by a troop of in-toxicated citizens, who had drowned their forrows in large bumpers, and, by their inebrity, were led to commit a number of ridiculous frolicks. One of them having engaged to difcover the profeſſion of every

paſſenger

paffenger by his external appearance, they had placed themfelves upon that fpot to obferve every one that went over the bridge, and the Count was unfortunately the firft that happened to come into their way.

He that was to guefs at the profeffion of the paffengers, was extremely puzzled by the Count's appearance; a wager of fome louis d'ors having been laid. He eafily conceived, notwithftanding the difguife of my friend, by his gait and fhape, that he was of a fuperior rank. He hefitated, therefore, fome moments to pronounce his opinions; croffing his arms, and gaping at the Count. The latter being ftruck by the oddity of that fcene, could not help fmiling, which infpired the drunken inquifitor with additional courage. He turned, therefore, to his comrades, who were diverted by his perplexity, exclaiming, "I will be d——d, if I don't guefs that gentleman's profeffion: I lay you one louis d'or more that he is a cuckold."

The

The whole company broke out into a
roaring laughter; and the decision of the
wager depending on the confession of the
other party, they preffed the poor Count,
in their merry humour, to confefs the fact.
My friend being armed with no other
weapon of defence, but a cane, was in
danger of being torn to pieces. He defended himfelf as well as he could; but,
without the affiftance of fome foldiers,
who came to his relief, he would probably have been forced to make the ridiculous confeffion.

Thus he was feafonably extricated from
the danger which had threatened him;
but, far from taking the whole affair for
what it really was, an accidental frolick,
he imagined it to have been pre-concerted,
to give him a hint of the infidelity of his
miftrefs; he fancied, at leaft, the whole
town was already informed of his cuck-
oldom. His blood began violently to
ferment, he quickened his fteps to the
houfe of his miftrefs, and entered her
apartment

apartment in the height of his paffion, abufing the poor, trembling girl with the bittereft reproaches. However, fhe foon collected herfelf; and having attempted in vain to foothe his rage, by tears and tender remonftrances, afked him, at length, coolly, "whether fhe fhould ring for her people, or whether he preferred to quit her houfe without their affiftance?" He chofe the latter; and fhe appeared the next day in public as the declared miftrefs of Baron de H******. This affair recurred, on the prefent occafion, to the recollection of my friend, and he imagined the Baron's malicious fmiles alluded to it. He went, therefore, to him, whifpering in his ear, "Baron, you will give me leave to afk you, how far *you* are concerned in this affair?"

The Baron made a low bow, replying, fmiling, in German, "My Lord, I fhall give you every explanation on that head you can wifh for."

The

The place where we were being not
proper for pushing the matter any farther,
the Count pretended to be satisfied with
this answer, and retired; yet I could
plainly see what was going on in his mind.
Caroline did every thing in her power to
make us forget the consequences of her
little caprice, displaying her mental charms
with a most bewitching humour, nature,
and elegance.  She endeavoured to dispel
the gloom which frowned on the Count's
brow, telling him, that she would try her
fortune with him the next day: however,
nothing was capable of restoring the harmony of his soul; and while I felt myself
as happy as a god by Caroline's side, and
reviewed all my ideas to select for her the
most natural and intelligible sentiments,
he was absorpt in a gloomy reverie, from
which he scarcely awoke now and then.

Supper was, at length, served up, and
we sat down to table in tolerable good
humour and harmony.  The conversation
turning on the siege of Gibraltar, the
company

company were defirous to know the particulars of it. The Count was requefted
to favour us with a circumftantial relation
of that remarkable fiege; but declined it
with a great deal of politenefs and modefty, directing the company to beg that
favour of Baron de H******, who had
given many proofs of his courage and fuperior talents on that occafion. The
Baron, having not the leaft fufpicion that
his conduct on that occafion was notorious,
accepted the challenge, with a prefump-
tuous fmile, as a juft tribute of his merits,
and began his narrative. I was aftonifhed
to hear with how much barefacednefs that
fellow interlarded his relation with a number of various adventures in which he
pretended to have been engaged. There
was no rencounter in which he had not
acted a principal part: he made the whole
company fhudder at the dangers which he
pretended to have experienced during the
war; and it was merely owing to his modefty and delicacy that he forbore to fpeak
alfo

alfo of thofe to which he was expofed by the fair fex. I am firmly convinced, that he flattered himfelf to have fold his rodo-montades for fterling truth, as he did not take the leaft notice of the fufpicious fmiles of the company, and would cer-tainly have carried his impudence ftill further, if the Count had not interrupted him at the conclufion of a moft romantic adventure with the words, " *And then you awoke?*" An audible whifper, which ran through the company when the Count ut-tered thefe farcaftic words, roufed him completely from his infatuation, and he ftopped half a minute, glowing with fhame and rage.

He then was going to vent his fury upon the Count, when the latter interrupted him with the greateft politenefs, turning to the company, and begging leave to re-late alfo an incident which happened at that time. The whole company fignified their approbation; but few only gueffed what was to come. The Count began his

ftory,

ſtory, directing ſome ſignificant looks at the Baron, who wanted to continue his tale, and only could be ſilenced by the general clamour of the company.

"When we raiſed the ſiege of Gibraltar," the Count reſumed, "moſt of thoſe who had expected to gain honor and preferment on that expedition as volunteers, abandoned every idea of making a new attempt; three of my comrades, and myſelf, reſigned on the ſpot, and went farther into the country, to recover from the fatigues of the campaign, and to viſit an intimate friend of mine, who had married a charming and rich Spaniſh lady. Our journey was more pleaſant than is uſual in Spain. Two of my companions, who reſembled me in their temper and good humour, as well as myſelf, found every where ſufficient opportunities for diverſion; and when nothing occurred that could afford us amuſement, the comical lies, and rodomontades, of our fourth fellow-traveller, made

made us forget the badnefs of the roads and the poverty of the inns.

" Don Antonio (thus we will call him) was one of the ftrangeft human beings nature has produced. He had a pretty good fhare of underftanding, and not little experience, but was of a moft fingu- lar difpofition. Although he knew that we had been eye witneffes of, and con- cerned in, almoft all engagements, in which he difplayed very little of the hero, yet he invented a number of adventures, in which he pretended to have acted a principal part, and endeavoured to per- fuade us of his veracity by a femblance of the greateft candour, as well as by num- berlefs oaths.

" Well invented!" we frequently ufed to exclaim, " though it is not true!" However, he pledged his honour, and, what was ftill more important, his tried courage, for the truth of his tale. We refolved, therefore, unanimoufly, to try,

on

on the next opportunity, how far we could rely upon the latter.

"Our common friend received us as well as we could expect, and did every thing in his power to prolong our ftay with him, and to give us pleafure. His country feat united all the charms of the Spanifh clime, and our rural diverfions were feafoned by the pleafant flows of humorous fallies. We played moft charming little tricks; and our fociable harmony prevented us from being offended when, now and then, our frolicks dege- nerated into fomething more than jeft. Our hoftefs and hoft foon knew Antonio's weak fide as well as we did; and we re- folved to repay him with a vengeance, on the firft opportunity, all the liberties he had taken with us, and foon were enabled to carry our purpofe into execution.

"A fudden noife arofe in the caftle, one night, while we were at fupper in a gar- den-houfe. Some of the fervants came running, pale and with ghaftly looks, to inform

inform our hoft fecretly, that a ghoft had been feen in one of the apartments. The Marquis acquainted us inftantly with that intelligence. The ladies grew deadly pale, and ftarted up from their chairs. Some gentlemen, who happily had fuc- ceeded to fupprefs the firft emotions of fear, began to raife a loud laughter, and to ridicule the cowardice of the fervants. The Marquis, however, declared the af- fair ought to be treated more ferioufly; ordered the fervants to light fome torches; and begging the ladies to keep themfelves quiet and eafy till his return, took up his fword, and begged us to follow him.

" Now a very tender fcene took place. The married ladies, as well as thofe of the unmarried, who had a lover amongft us, began folemnly to proteft againft that refolution, and conjured us not to leave them unprotected. The Marquis, how- ever, entreated them to give him leave not to fuffer himfelf to be robbed thus quietly; and, after a number of remonftrances, admonitions,

admonitions, and obfecrations, had been exchanged, it was agreed to examine the affair in the company of the ladies. The latter took fearfully hold of the arms of their neighbours, the fervants led the way with a blaze of torches, and we covered the proceffion with drawn fwords.

"I did not rightly know what to think of the matter, which appeared to me to be rather ftrange, and quite unpre-con-certed. It was impoffible to draw any conclufion from the looks of our hoft. He really feemed to be rather agitated, and I knew that he was but a poor dif-fembler. I alfo could not imagine that he wantonly would alarm a whole com-pany, merely to punifh an individual. I concluded, therefore, that really fome-thing muft have happened; and giving, at that time, very little credit to the ap-parition of ghofts, fufpected fome roguery, and refolved to behave with as much cou-rage as my unhappy education would al-low in that point.

Vol. III.          D          "I grew,

"I grew, at length, fo tranquil and cool, that I was capable of making obfervations on the company. At firft, a general, profound, and anxious filence prevailed amongft us, and was only now and then interrupted by a folitary figh, which efcaped fome of our companions. Don Antonio uttered, at length, the greateft oath he could find in the vifible agony of his mind. His fair neighbour (for he had carefully avoided to offer his arm to one of the ladies, in order to be at full liberty to take to his heels in cafe of neceffity) conjured him to be quiet. However, he probably miftook this for a challenge to regale the company with fome more of his fine exclamations, and repeated every oath he knew, to proteft that he was impatient to have the pleafure of engaging a ghoft. Yet, notwithftanding thefe ftrong proteftations, he could not help looking fearfully around now and then, and keeping carefully between the two fervants who clofed the train. He even made, at intervals,

intervals, a certain noife with his teeth, which is not accounted to be a token of heroifm, when the wind ruftled a little ftronger betwixt the leaves, and became more and more filent the nearer we approached the caftle. The reft of the company were alfo not entirely free of fearful apprehenfions; and there was not one who did not exhibit ftronger or weaker fymptoms of anxious apprehenfions.

" A fudden guft of wind, which extinguifhed fome of the torches, ferved to encreafe the fear which prevailed in our heroic fociety: and fome of the ladies protefted they would not advance a ftep farther, if they were not lighted again immediately. We were, therefore, obliged to halt, which happening frequently, our march was very much retarded; and thofe that were more fearful than the reft, gained time to communicate their apprehenfions to their neighbours, and to infect even the fervants, who, at firft, had difplayed pretty much courage.

D 2 " We

"We arrived, at length, at the caftle-
gate. The haunted apartment was on the
firft floor; but the anxiety of the company
difplayed itfelf already at the ftaircafe
which led to the great hall. Numberlefs
fears and apprehenfions exhibited themfelves on the countenances of my fellow-
adventurers, which were rendered more
vifible by their painful exertions to conceal them from the reft. We now counted
the company, to fee whether none had
ftayed behind; and were ftruck with aftonifhment, on finding that the Chevalier
Antonio was miffing. We were already
going to ridicule his cowardice feverely,
and felt ourfelves ftrongly inclined to
laugh at the defertion of his vaunted courage, when he convinced us that we had
wronged him; for he came running out
of breath, and wiping the fweat from his
face. He even afked, with a great clamour,
why we did not proceed; and the whole
company being re-animated with new
courage

courage by his noify exhortations, advanced towards the great ftaircafe.

" But now a new difficulty arofe; none of us being willing or able to afcend the fteps firft. The Marquis was retained by his lady, and the reft were ftopt by his example. At length, fhe fuffered him to proceed, after he had afked her angrily, whether fhe took him for a child; and Antonio, who was in the rear, had exclaimed, Why we did not go on? He now afcended the ftairs; and myfelf, with a friend of mine, who had taken me by the arm, pufhed through the reft, and followed him clofely, while the greater part of the company were loitering partly at the bottom, and partly in the middle, of the ftaircafe, according to their refpective fhare of courage. We did not mind their backwardnefs, and proceeded towards the haunted apartment with a great fhow of courage, but I dare fay not without palpitating hearts.

D 3

," The

" The fervants, who carried the torches, being in the rear, I went back to provide myfelf with one. The whole troop, who followed us flowly, watching every ftep of ours, were put in motion by my hafty return ; and fome, who were already at the landing-place, put themfelves in motion to turn back on the firft fignal. I could not help fmiling at the fear of men who had fought like lions before Gibraltar, faced all the dangers and hardfhips of that fatal fiege with coolnefs and bravery, and now were overcome fo much by the prejudices of their religion and education, as to give way to a moft extraordinary and childifh fear. Inftead of being infected by their example, I derived additional courage from their unmanly conduct, returned laughing to my friend, and opening the door for the Marquis, went before him with a torch.

" However, we ftarted a few fteps back, feized with terror, as foon as we had entered the apartment; and the reft

of

of the company, who were awaiting the
event, hurried inftantly down ftairs. Before two feconds were elapfed, we were
forfaken by the whole train, except a fervant of the Marquis, who was uncommonly attached to his mafter, and would
not leave him in the danger which feemed
to threaten us. The fight which we beheld was, indeed, terrible enough. An
enormous figure, with large, fiery eyes,
advanced towards us; and I do not know
whether an antecedent tranfitory fright
does not fharpen the fenfes and the judgment; for I made, almoft immediately, an
obfervation which confiderably diminifhed
my fear.

"Firft of all, the figure was too gro-
tefque. What a moderate deception
would have effected, is generally fruftra-
ted by an extravagant one. I could not
help remarking that the figure refembled
the giant who challenged Don Quixote,
the celebrated knight of the woeful countenance. This laughable idea, which

D 4                                    forced

forced itfelf upon my mind, made me
fufpect the whole; for as foon as I advanced further with my torch, I perceived
a fecond figure, fneaking into an adjoin-
ing apartment, which communicated with
thofe of the Marchionefs that bordered
on the garden. The room in which we
were was a ftate-chamber of the Marquis.
This train of ideas came almoft in a moment in my mind; and looking around, I
miffed a filver clock which ufed to ftand
on a table. Having feen it in its place
before we went to fupper, I could eafily
account for the apparition.

   "I took, therefore, our dubious hoft
by the arm, exclaiming, "They are
thieves, as true as I am alive! Don't you
fee that your clock is gone?" He was
ftruck by that remark, and we inftantly
attacked the phantom with drawn fwords.
However, the human fpectre had a long
ftaff in its hand, with which it parried our
thrufts excellently. The fervant entering
with a candle, along with my friend, I
                              obferved

obferved that the torch which I ftill held in my left hand was in my way, and threw it into my antagonift's face. His head-drefs caught fire; and I threw my fword down, taking hold of his ftick. The Marquis did the fame: we began to embrace him in a moft violent manner, and before half a minute was elapfed, came with him down upon the floor. The fellow being feized with defpair, difplayed a more than human ftrength, and could have killed every one of us if he had been armed. Being, however, engaged by four men at once, he was foon exhaufted; and begged us, in a hollow accent, to fpare him. The Marquis promifed o pardon him; and he confeffed that he belonged to a band of five robbers, who had intended to avail themfelves of the buftle our feftival produced in the caftle, to plunder it: in fhort, he confirmed my fufpicion.

"His hands were tied, and he was committed to the guard of the fervants. The

D 5                    Marquis

Marquis and my friend examined every
apartment, in order to apprehend the rest
of the gang; and I went down stairs to
send some servants to their assistance. A
death-like silence reigned every where,
and not one human being was to be seen.
They even had left some candles upon the
stairs, to effect their escape with more
ease. At the bottom of the staircase I
found a lady who had been left there in a
swoon; and a little farther I discovered
Don Antonio in a condition that was not
much better. As soon as he heard a noise
on the stairs, he covered his face with his
handkerchief, and expected a happy de-
liverance, seized with a most painful
agony."

"Prepare thyself for eternity, Don Antonio!" I exclaimed, on coming nearer;
"for thou must die!"

"Spare me, O! spare me only this
time!" he stammered, in a hollow and
broken accent, which scarcely was intelligible.

"No

"No mercy this time!" I replied laughing, in my natural accent. He knew me inftantly, took the handkerchief from his face, and gazing at me with aftoniſhment, ſaid, highly rejoiced, "Dear Count, is it you? are you ſtill alive? You have played me a fine trick."

"I now gave him a brief account of the whole affair, and recommended the fainting lady to his care. This animated him at once with new life, and he haſtened to her with the alacrity of a buck to lend his affiſtance.

"I found the ſervants diſperſed in different parts of the garden, and called to them to affiſt their maſter. The reſt of the company were returned to the garden-houſe, and there awaited the event in great anxiety. When I entered the door, the ladies ſat up a loud ſcream, becauſe they did not at firſt know me, and miſtook me for the ghoſt. I never beheld a more ſingular ſcene than that. Every diſtinction of rank and ſex was ſuſpended for a while.

D 6                    The

The general panic having driven the whole
company into a corner of the faloon, the
coyeft ladies fat upon the lap of their
lovers; the moft obftinate fhrew clung
round the neck of her patient hufband,
and the bittereft enemies and rivals held
one another enfolded in their arms in the
moft amicable manner.

"At length, they perceived their miftake, joyfully exclaiming, with one voice,
" It is the Count! it is the Count!"

"It is impoffible to defcribe the aftonifhment and the rapture with which I
was received; not fo much on my account,
than becaufe they faw themfelves relieved
from their apprehenfions. I gave them a
brief account of the affair; and when I
had finifhed my report, the Chevalier
joined us with the lady whom I had recommended to his care.

"Was the Chevalier alfo prefent?" one
of the company exclaimed.

"Moft certainly; he acted a principal
part," I replied.

"This

" This made Don Antonio fuppofe that
I had not yet related the incident; he
therefore took my affertion for a compli-
ment paid to his courage, bowed, and began, with the greateft impudence, to relate the affair, with fome additions and
embellifhments of his own invention.
We liftened patiently to his tale: however,
the Marquis had mean time entered the
faloon, and hearing his rodomontades,
was ftruck with his barefaced impudence.
He took his refolution on the fpot, and
winking me to follow him into the garden,
communicated a plan to me, which was
to make Don Antonio fpend the night in
a different manner than he feemed to
expect.

"Our meafures were foon taken; and we
had only to give a hint to the Marchionefs, in which I fortunately fucceeded on
my return into the faloon. She comprehended me fo quickly, and fo completely,
that I concluded we only anticipated her
defign; thus much had Antonio exafperated

rated the company by his barefaced
fictions.

" Our return restored cheerfulnefs and
merriment to our fociable circle.  We fat
gaily down to the defert, ridiculing one
another for our fear, and the heroes of the
drama earned the deferved applaufe.  Nothing makes people more daring than a
danger which has been happily overcome.
There was not one amongft us who could
not have defied all the infernal fpirits; and
but very few who did not loudly declaim
againft the exiftence of apparitions, as we
had been fortunate enough to have difcovered the human nature of one.  It may
eafily be conceived who was the moft clamorous amongft us.  Don Antonio fwore
that he had laughed immoderately at our
childifh fear, that he had wanted to make
game at me when I came down, and had
been alarmed by nothing in the world
than the fituation of the lady.

" Our hoftefs now interrupted him, declaring, that her education, as well as a

certain

certain circumſtance, did not allow her to coincide with the opinion moſt of the company ſeemed to have adopted. Every one being curious to know that circumſtance, ſhe was preſſed to relate it; upon which ſhe proteſted that it was no ſecret, that, every night, at twelve o'clock, ſuch a terrible noiſe was heard in the chapel of the caſtle, that one expected it would be turned upſide down. The Marquis raiſed a loud laugh, in which he was joined by the whole company, but particularly by Don Antonio, who, probably recollecting that midnight was already paſt, propoſed to the company to go with him into the chapel. However, the Marchioneſs diſſembled to pay no attention to what he ſaid, and feigned to be offended by the ridicule which her information had been received with; declaring, that ſhe would lay any wager, that none of the gentlemen who were pleaſed to laugh at her, would fetch a fan ſhe had left in her pew in the afternoon.

" A general

" A general filence of fome feconds was
the confequence of this declaration. The
Marquis, at length, thought proper to interrupt it, declaring, that he would cheerfully accept the wager, and that he was
firmly perfuaded any one of the gentlemen prefent would render her that fervice
inftantly with the greateft pleafure. We
all confirmed his declaration, and begged
the Marchionefs to choofe her hero. She
now furveyed the whole circle, and Don
Antonio always turned pale when fhe
feemed to be going to fix upon him. Her
looks were, to his greateft joy, feveral
times fixed upon me; yet poor Antonio
had, at length, the misfortune to be fin-
gled out by her. The Chevalier being
bound by his word of honour, could not
but accept the charge, and thank her for
her good opinion of him. Having once
more ftolen a clandeftine look at his watch,
and convinced himfelf that it was near
two o'clock, he took his fword, and left
us with a very martial air. Yet his courage

rage failed him already at the door.
Having inadvertently unfaftened the red
cockade of his hat, it fell into his face.
He was violently frightened; but when we
began to laugh, and declared that it was a
bad omen, he collected himfelf again,
and looking at us with an indefcribable
contempt, on account of our fuppofed
timidity, flung the cockade into a corner. We took it up, refolving to make a
good ufe of it. He had no fooner quitted
the faloon, than the Marquis communicated his plan and meafures to the company, afking the gentlemen which of them
would act a part in the farce he was going
to play? Don Joachim F******, a man
like a giant, and Don Romero L******,
who was rather of a dwarfifh ftature, offered inftantly to act the principal parts.
Our plan now was briefly concerted, and
the company rofe to follow the Chevalier
at a diftance, and, if poffible, to get the
ftart of him."

" Never

"Never has a plan better fucceeded. The fky was indeed overclouded; however, it was not fo dark that we could not have difcerned the objects at fome diftance; and we could clearly perceive that Don Antonio anxioufly liftened at every bufh before he approached it, and that his fteps grew flower and flower, the nearer he came to the wall of the church-yard. He brandifhed his fword to frighten away the fpirits, and at length arrived at the gate of the church-yard. He opened it with a great noife, and fhut it again in the fame violent manner. He, at the fame time, began to fing and to whiftle with all his might, ftruck againft all the croffes that came in his way; but foon loft his way, and ftumbled over one tomb-ftone after the other, which enabled us to fteal into the chapel from the oppofite fide about ten minutes before his arrival. Having miffed the large gate, it was almoft impof-fible for him to come to the pew of the

Marchionefs,

Marchionefs, becaufe he would have been obliged to climb over all the other feats.

" There was only one lady in our company, who, however, had almoft fpoiled the whole fport. For when fhe faw the poor Chevalier climbing over the pews, and heard him groan in a moft rueful accent, fhe broke out into an immoderate laughter, and endeavouring to ftifle it, rendered it only more hideous. I had placed myfelf near the organ; and being at a lofs how to remedy the fault fhe had committed, accompanied her with a ftill more difharmonious paffage on the inftrument. This produced an effect which furpaffed my moft fanguine expectation, as but little wind was in the bellows, and I never was an adept in mufic.

." The poor Chevalier was almoft petrified. He fat down in a pew, and awaited, in a kind of ftupefaction, the things that were to come. I am fure he would have cared neither for the fan nor for his reputation, if he had had the leaft hope of getting
fafe

safe out of the chapel. In this diftrefs
he looked anxioufly about for an afylum,
and feeing fomething of·a white colour,
which were the pillars of the pulpit, fhine
through the dufk, that prevailed around
him, he climbed over the remaining pews
to get at that fuppofed place of fafety.

" We thought it our duty to light him
on that expedition. A great electric machine, which the Marquis had ordered to
be placed near the pulpit, ferved our purpofe excellently, emitting from the conductor, at firft, large fparks, and then a
whole electric ftream. We alfo lighted
fome candles of the large chandelier,
which was fufpended in the centre of the
chapel, by means of a quantity of hemp,
which was overfpread with fulphur and
pitch. However, we foon extinguifhed
the candles again. Two fervants, who were
ftationed at the church-yard, broke fome
panes of glafs, which came with a great
noife into the chapel: the doors were
opened and fhut again; the howling of
cats

cats was imitated; fome of the company
blew a ftrong current of air into his face
by means of large bellows; the fhrill
found of whiftles re-echoed from every
corner; and as the effect of the electrical
machine grew ftronger, whole ftreams of
fire illuminated the chapel at intervals.
We alfo had contrived to tie cords round
his arms and legs, which made the poor
fellow believe that he was fpell-bound.
In fhort, the effect of our contrivance was
fo great, that the actors themfelves could
not help fhuddering now and then.

" Mean time, a thick fmoke arofe near
the altar, and Don Joachim F****** and
Don Romero L****** ftepped forth from
its grifly womb, dreffed like devils. The
latter being of a very diminutive fize,
made the former appear a great deal more
gigantic than he really was. The garments of either were ftreaked with phof-
phorus; and Don Joachim F****** carried a large lanthorn on his head, on which
was written, " *Sinner, prepare thyfelf, for*
*thou*

*thou muſt die!"* Don Romero had the cockade which Don Antonio had flung on the ground, and now was ſtained with phoſphorus, fixed to his head. Both of them extended two long fiery arms, the extremities of which were armed with claws, and howled ſome hollow accents. Antonio ſhut his eyes when he ſaw theſe two frightful figures, and did not open them for ſome minutes.

" However, the ſcene was ſoon changed to our mutual terror. The pulpit-door opened; a man, clad in a white robe, armed with a large croſs, and carrying a lanthorn, ſtept forth. He was ſoon followed by one more, clad in black.

" It was the paſtor of the place, and the ſexton, who had heard the uproar in the chapel. The Marquis having neglected to inform them of our nocturnal undertaking, they were come to ſee what was the matter. We ſoon knew them; however, the two diſguiſed devils, who never had ſeen them before, imagined

that

that they were apparitions from another world, their late fear feized them again, and they ran with all poffible fpeed towards the door. They had, however, the misfortune to lofe their way between the pews; Don Joachim's lanthorn dropt from his head, and fell in Don Romero's face; the one was frightened at the other; yet the latter had the prefence of mind to take it up, to faften it to one of his long artificial arms, which he took upon his fhoulder, and thus happily gained the door. His giant-like affiftant was clofe at his heels.

" But now a new misfortune happened; for when the prieft began his exorcifms, both of them were tempted to look once more back; the little one, who led the way, turning fuddenly round, knocked the lanthorn fo. violently into the face of his tall companion, that the latter, imagining to have received a blow from a fpirit, dropped half dead upon the ground. Don Romero was terribly frightened at

4                    that

that incident, but retained fufficient recollection to difencumber himfelf of every
thing that could retard him on his flight,
and to leap with the greateft agility over
the graves. Yet the terror which pervaded his agitated mind did not leave him
fufficient power to proceed far, and he
feated himfelf, at length, half fainting,
upon a tombftone, patiently awaiting the
event.

" The Marquis now refolved to put an
end to the whole fcene; and making a
fignal to the fervants, the machinery was
concealed as well as poffible; every one of
the actors ftole filently out of the chapel,
and the whole company met at the great
gate. The firft thing we did was to reftore Don Joachim to the ufe of his fenfes;
Don Romero foon joined us; and having
lighted our torches, we repaired again to
the chapel.

" The prieft was ftill preaching. He
had taken the candle out of the lanthorn,
and fixed it upon the pulpit, devoutly
reading

reading the exorcifms from his book.
The Marquis now ftepped before the pulpit, afking the prieft what his ftrange behaviour meant, if he was in his fenfes, or
had loft his underftanding? Yet he remained fome time longer in his error;
and recollecting, at length, the voice of
his mafter, was feized with amazement,
and gave us a brief account of his tran-
factions. The Marquis then begged him
to go home, and we haftened to affift the
poor Chevalier.

" We were ftruck with terror on perceiving not the leaft fign of life in him.
His pulfe ceafed to beat, and the Marquis
repented already the whole affair, thinking
to have carried the jeft rather too far, when
the poor fellow, at once, opened his eyes to
our greateft joy. Yet he ftill fancied to
be in the power of fpirits, and cried aloud
for affiftance. We fcarcely could convince
him that we were human beings, and
come in queft of him. He now was carried to the caftle, and put to bed; having

VOL. III.        E        entirely

entirely loft the ufe of his fpeeçh. When
we vifited him the next morning, we
found him quite reftored, and he informed
us that he had fallen afleep at chapel, and
had a terrible dream."

Here the Count concluded his tale,
which we had liftened to with the greateft
pleafure, though moft of us had heard it
already, and knew very well who the perfon was whom he had introduced under the
name of Antonio. The Baron was covered with fhame, and had loft the power
of utterance, yet was prudent enough to
fupprefs his wrath.

What rendered the whole tale moft en-
tertaining, was the prefence of Don Romero L******, a man of known courage,
honefty, and of an excellent temper, who
made no fecret of his defects; and, at the
clofe of the hiftory, exclaimed, "By holy
Peter! I was terribly frightened."

"Then you alfo was prefent on that occafion?" one of the company afked,
laughing.

"Yes!

" Yes! yes!" he refumed; "and the Baron yonder, too, was not far off."

The laughter encreafed. However, the Baron thought it proper to bridle his paffions, and not to reply a fyllable, but to wait for a more favourable opportunity to revenge himfelf upon the Count, which he very nearly had found that very night.

We now converfed a little longer on different fubjects, and then parted, as it feemed, entirely reconciled to one another. The Count faw Caroline to her carriage, and foon after went home with me, to all appearance completely happy.

He was ufed to fit every night half an hour with me on my fofa, and to converfe on the occurrences of the day; but that time his mind was fo much occupied with the paft events, that he forgot it, and went directly to his apartment, which occafioned one of the drolleft fcenes of my life.

To make myfelf perfectly underftood, I muft premife a brief defcription of the

arrangement

arrangement of our houfe. The ground
floor was occupied by our landlady, a
mantua-maker; the firft floor was inhabited by the Count and myfelf; and my
fervants lodged in the fecond floor. Our
landlady was a young, gay woman, who
underftood her profeffion excellently, and
made the utmoft of every little advantage.
She not only let the remaining apartments
of the ground floor to compaffionate ladies, but her charitable difpofition was fo
great, that fhe alfo admitted fome young
gentlemen by day and night to her own
room. The Count and myfelf being very
much difpleafed with her conduct, we had
taken a refolution to quit her houfe the
fubfequent week.

The Baron had vifited us fometimes,
and taken a liking to our little gay landlady. He was not ufed to flip an opportunity of ingratiating himfelf with the ladies; yet our hoftefs did not think proper
to be kind to the Baron; and fome weeks
elapfed before he could make any confiderable

derable advances in her favour, notwithftanding the great pains he took to make
her favourably difpofed to him. But
learning, at length, that two floors in her
houfe foon would be evacuated, he paid
for that which the Count inhabited before-
hand, and, in return, put himfelf in poffeffion of the happinefs he had been hunting after for fome time. He paid, that
very night, a vifit to his future landlady;
and was fafely houfed in her bed when the
adventure occurred which I now am going
to relate.

## CHAPTER IV.

THE reader will recollect that the
Count, on our return from the card-
party, went immediately into his own
apartment, inftead of fitting half an hour
with me as he was ufed to do. Having
undreffed himfelf, he obferved that it was
too early to go to bed: he, therefore,
flung himfelf upon his fofa, to reflect on

the occurrences of the day, and his affair with the Baron. His blood being in a violent fermentation, he tormented himself for some time with ruminating on the bad consequences the latter might produce. Yet the association of ideas at length brought him back again to Caroline; he wandered from one smiling reverie to the other, and at laft fell afleep.

His fituation being, however, not very eafy, he awoke after he had flept about half an hour. In his drowfinefs he imagined to have refted on my fofa as ufual, took up his candle, and wifhed me a good night, fuppofing that I was gone to bed. He went foftly down ftairs, and thus came to the apartment where the mantua-maker was fallen faft afleep in the arms of her new paramour, and, notwithftanding his perceiving fome change in the furniture, yet he ftill imagined to be in his own apartment, and was aftonifhed at his heavy drowfinefs, which, as he thought, reprefented every object in a
different

different manner to his eyes. He now began to undrefs himfelf, opened the curtains, and placed the table with the candle near the bed, to extinguifh it when he fhould have gone to bed. But unfortunately one of the Baron's boots laying on the floor, he put one foot of the table upon it, the candle dropped down, and fell burning into the face of the former. The Baron awoke with a terrible fcream; and it may eafily be conceived how much the Count was aftonifhed to fee his bed occupied by his mortal enemy. Being of a very irafcible temper, his aftonifhment was turned into the moft violent rage at that fuppofed impertinence. He uttered a dreadful oath, and ran to the corner in which he had placed his fword; but being not able to find it, he rung with fuch a vehemence for his fervants, that the ftring of the bell broke; for being at a lofs to account for that incident, he was determined to chaftife the Baron in an exemplary manner.

E 4 The

The latter had, mean time, haftened
out of the bed, and found his fword.
Thinking that the Count was his rival, he
congratulated himfelf upon the favourable
opportunity, he imagined to have, to get
rid of him at once;. and while his fair
companion fcreamed with all her might,
went in his fhirt to attack the poor Count,
who held his breeches in one hand, and
with the other, which was armed with the
Baron's cane, parried his antagonift's
thrufts with the greateft difficulty. Yet
being an excellent fencer, he foon attacked
his adverfary in an offenfive manner, without recollecting that his weapon was only
a wooden one, beat the Baron's fword out
of his hand, and gave him fuch a violent
blow on his ftomach, that he began to
roar in a moft rueful accent.

The lady, who had not ceafed fcreaming
all the time the combat lafted, imagined
that her Adonis could not but have received fome material hurt by the Count's
furious blows, acccmpanied the vocifera-
tion

tion of her charmer with additional force,
which roufed every inhabitant of the houfe
that had not been awakened by the Count's
violent ringing of the bell. A number of
people appeared, by degrees, in the apartment, in their fhirts, and feemed to be
very much inclined to affift the landlady.
Some fpits and pokers began already to
approach the Count, when my coachman
entered the room with his horfe-whip.
Being of a giant-like ftature, which was
not inferior to his bodily ftrength, he could
look over the heads of the reft, and foon
perceived the Count's diftrefsful fituation.
He, therefore, began to lay about him with
his whip, and handled the naked figures
fo unmercifully, that the conteft was terminated in a moment. The affailants
dropt their arms, and faved themfelves as
well as they could.

The Count feeing himfelf delivered
from his aggreffors, began to reflect a little, and perceived that he was not in his
own apartment. The fcreaming lady in

E 5 the

the bed now attracted his attention, and
he went to take her out. No fooner did
he behold her face, and fee who fhe was,
than he gueffed at the real ftate of the
whole affair. Want of gallantry being
not on the lift of his defects, he thought
it was his duty to excufe his fatal miftake,
and to foothe the wrath of the offended
fair one. He, therefore, told her a number of fweet things, excufing himfelf as
well as he could; and feeing many inviting charms, difencumbered of every
envious covering, before him, embraced
her at laft.

In that very moment I entered the
apartment, armed with a fword, carrying
a candle, and accompanied by all the fervants, who were armed in the fame manner, the Count's valet having waked me
as foon as he had miffed his mafter. A
more ridiculous fcene never has been wit-
neffed. On ftepping out of my apartment, I had met fome fhopmen, who
were half naked, and took to their heels as
                                    foon

foon as they faw me. When I came to the lady's apartment, I faw the coachman ftanding on the threfhold, gazing into the room, and holding his fides with laughing. The Baron ftood in the centre of the apartment in the fame pofture, which, however, feemed to be owing to a different caufe; and the Count fat by the bed, ca- reffing and, at laft, tenderly embracing, a lady that was almoft entirely naked. The latter glowed with a high crimfon hue, but the fire that burned in her face was not the effect of anger. Her longing eyes furveyed the beautiful form of the' Count; fhe fuffered his kiffes, and ap- peared to be difpleafed with nothing but the number of witneffes. Seeing me, at length, at the head of the fervants, fhe ejaculated a loud fcream, and difengaging herfelf from the Count's embraces, hid herfelf in the bed.

The firft thing I did, was to fly to the affiftance of the poor Baron. The Count, who laughed immoderately, affifted me
faithfully;

faithfully; but our creft fallen hero was in
fuch agonizing pains, that he fcarcely
could fpeak. He complained of violent
pains, and a great quantity of congealed
blood had gathered on the place where he
was wounded. I fent inftantly for a furgeon, and affifted my friend in putting on
his cloaths. The lady in the bed declaring that it was impoffible he could remain
in her apartment, we carried him into a
coach, and faw him to his lodgings,
where we committed him to the care of
his fervants.

We took the greateft pains to keep the
whole tranfaction private; however, this
was impoffible; for it was circulated
through the whole town the next morning.
We received every where congratulations,
and were obliged to relate all the particulars of that ftrange incident. The Baron
was no fooner able to go abroad, than
the Count received a challenge, in which
the choice of arms was entirely left to his
option; and he was generous enough to
fix

fix upon piftols. Time and place were
agreed upon. The Count feemed to pre-
fage a fatal cataftrophe; having made his
will, and committed it to my care, he
bade a tender adieu to all his friends, under
the pretext of a little journey. Caroline
too was not forgotten. He imagined no
one knew any thing of the real nature of
his pretended journey; yet I could plainly
perceive that his friends looked upon this
journey as his laft, at all events. Caroline
almoft fainted, on rifing from the fofa, to
offer him her beautiful hand for a farewell
kifs. My rifing jealoufy perceived this
plainly, and it did alfo not efcape her that
the Count obferved it too with great
emotion.

We left town early in the morning on
horfeback, and found the Baron and his
fecond already on the appointed fpot.
Neither of the two antagonifts being a
great markfman, each of them had brought
two braces of piftols with him, which
were charged by the feconds, and then
exchanged.

exchanged. The fteps were meafured, and they took their proper diftance. Five fhots were already fired without any effect. The Baron aimed fo miferably, that he almoft had wounded me, though I was more than fix paces diftant from the Count. I therefore called to him, when he was going to fire again, "not to tremble fo- much." He was, however, but too fuccefsful; for the Count dropt on the ground, exclaiming that he was wounded in the fide. I haftened to affift him, and faw the blood gufh violently from his wound. The Baron too offered to affift my friend; but the Count waved his hand, defiring him to flee as faft as poffible. The Baron feemed really to be very much affected; and having embraced the Count and myfelf, mounted his horfe, and rode away with his fecond. If the Count had been killed on the fpot, I fhould probably have made a better ufe of the remaining brace of piftols than my friend. But feeing a chance of faving his life, I was too much

much occupied with a defire of giving
him relief, as to entertain any idea of
vengeance.

I flattered myfelf with the hope that the
wound was not mortal, the ball not having
penetrated deep enough as to injure his
inteftines materially. I only apprehended
the violent effufion of blood might prove
fatal to him. Having dreffed his wound
as well as poffible with the affiftance of
my fervant, we carried him to a neighbouring village. The furgeon was of my
opinion, and the event confirmed my
hope; for a few weeks confinement and
reft cured him completely.

I could not prevent the duel, and the
danger of the Count, from being known
amongft our friends at Paris; and that
incident gave us an opportunity of perceiving that we had a great many who
really wifhed us well. All of them difplayed the moft anxious defire of feeing
him, and of contributing fomething towards his recovery. The ladies, in particular,

ticular, fcarcely left our houfe; and when he began to mend perceptibly, we began again to recommence our jocund affemblies with our ufual gaiety. Caroline alfo vifited at our houfe under the protection of an old uncle, and feemed to be particularly rejoiced at the Count's amendment.

One evening we were fitting at table, partaking of a cheerful fupper. The Count had declared that day that he intended to leave his apartment on the fubfequent one, and we were talking of a little feaft which was to be given on that occafion. No one was more happy at it than Caroline. She fat oppofite to me, and I could plainly perceive the expreffions of her fecret joy on her glowing countenance. I was abforpt in the contemplation of her charms, and felt my heart beat in unifon with hers. I was thrilled with a fecret pleafure, which, however, was mixed with fomething very bitter.

bitter. How nice is the perception of a lover's fenfes!

At once fhe grew pale; her large blue eyes, which were fparkling with rapture, gazed joyfully amazed at the door which was behind me; her fork dropt upon the floor; fhe held her napkin before her face, and leaned a little back againft the chair. I was juft going to her affiftance, when every face was turned towards the door. The chairs were fuddenly overturned; every one left the table; a confufed clamour filled the apartment; and turning my head, feized with aftonifhment, I beheld the Count enfolded in the arms of friendfhip.

What a feaft for us to fee him thus unexpectedly amongft us! We all received him as a loft and fuddenly recovered treafure; the tendereft careffes were lavifhed upon him, but the moft expreffive endearments were only weak emblems of our ecftatic joy. He returned them faintly; but the languoúr which his words and

motions

expreſſed only ſerved to animate them
with additional ardor. We placed him in
the middle; but no cuſhion was deemed
ſoft enough, no chair commodious enough,
to ſeat the dear, recovered fugitive upon.
A general ſatisfaction prevailed in our
joyous circle; he was the monarch to
whom our hearts paid a willing, cheerful
homage. Caroline ſeated herſelf, at length,
with a charming ſimplicity, by his ſide, to
nurſe the dear idol of our hearts. He
was deeply affected by her angelic good-
neſs, but could not find words to expreſs
his feelings.

Wit and humour now returned to our
circle in an overflowing meaſure, and with
additional gaiety. The graces mingled
with our ſociety, and the god of cheerful
hilarity preſided at our table. Our con-
verſation overflowed with witty ſallies; a
general deſire of giving pleaſure to our
darling pervaded every boſom. The
Count's cheerfulneſs was of a more gentle
complexion; he ſmiled only when we
laughed.

laughed.    Caroline animated him with
half concealed and half vifible careffes,
and the warmth of friendfhip foon blazed
perceptibly up in the flame of love. Every
member of our happy fociety was charmed
with the dear object of our love, and applauded his enchanting ideas; I alone fat
mute, and, at the fight of his happinefs,
felt myfelf confumed by a fecret fire, for
which I neither could nor would account.

Here begins a period of my life, on
which I cannot reflect without defpifing
myfelf; in which I was mifled by a glowing paffion to forget every thing that was
dear to me, and that I ever fhould have
held facred.    And, gracious Heaven!
what a paffion? Not that of a firft love, in
which the heated blood urges us to facrifice all prejudices, and every idea that op-
pofes our defires; it was not that love
which boldly breaks all the fetters of human nature, and even tears all other fofter
ties; no, it was a paffion kindled by jealoufy after the *firft* bloom of life was paft,
and

and numberlefs painful experiences ought
to have put me on my guard, after love
even had lavifhed all her bleffings on me;
a hopelefs, unhappy paffion, inflamed by
impoffibility, and combating the moft
facred duties. What a misfortune is it to
*have been* for fome time the favourite of
fortune! Nothing had been able to refift
me as yet, but here was the boundary of
my power; and while I attempted to over-
leap it, I was in danger to lofe a friend,
a real treafure, in the purfuit of an ima-
ginary one.

I was the only perfon in our cheerful
circle that did not fincerely fhare the
general flow of pleafure which pervaded
the heart of every one prefent. The fmile
of cheerfulnefs fat on my lips, but baneful poifon rankled in my heart. My eyes,
which fcarcely were able to retain the tear
of painful difappointment, were overclouded with a mift. Every innocent
glance of Caroline's looks, meeting thofe
of the enraptured Count, ftung me to the
heart;

heart; every tender gesture of hers threatened to choke me. I laughed immoderately, to conceal the real cause of the big tears that started from my heavy eyes, and to disguise the visible agitation of my bosom.

Yet my strange alteration did not escape the Count's keen sightedness. He now took a too small share in the general flow of pleasure as not to be a good observer, and repeatedly extended his hand to me over the table to reconcile me to him. I accepted, but could not have squeezed it for the world. My cheerfulness was so unnatural, so extravagant, that I am astonished it did not strike the whole company.

" Dear Marquis," said he, as soon as we were left to ourselves, " dear Marquis, what ails you?"

I had squeezed myself into a corner of the sofa, absorpt in a profound reverie, averting my weeping eyes from the Count, and turning them towards the window, through which the pale light of the moon trembled.

trembled. A melancholy train of gloomy
fcenes of former times, as it were, paffed
vifibly the review before my overclouded
eyes, and I compared the overflowing
meafure of my fufferings with the fcanty
portion of my joys. Only the prefent
moment fways in our mind in fuch a difpofition, and reflects its hue on fufferings
and pleafures paft, on our wifhes and fears,
on our hopes and expectations. Feathers
fink to the bottom when the torrent is too
violent, and rocks are unrooted. In that
moment the whole courfe of my life appeared to me to have been deftitute of
every joy, and futurity ftared me grifly
in the face. Without being rightly confcious of the original fource of that agonizing ftate of mind, every expectation
was thereby infected, and every cheering
hope deftroyed at once. No fituation of
mind is fo dreadful as the moment in
which a violent, hopelefs paffion, which
we have ftruggled with in vain, convulfes
every faculty of the foul in its firft incon-

fcious

fcious rife. I fcarcely heard the Count's queftion, yet the dubious fhake of his head did not efcape my notice.

" You don't hear me, dear Carlos!" he refumed. " I fear you are not well?"

" Indeed, I believe you are right," I replied mechanically; " for I feel fomething here," pointing to the left fide.

The Count laughed at that gefture, affumed a cheerful air, and faid, " So much the worfe, Carlos; for hurts on that fide are generally incurable." He expected I fhould fall in with his merry humour; yet I was entirely mute, and he refumed again:

" Tell me, for Heaven's fake, Marquis, what is the matter with you. You are entirely changed; or do you think that I have not feen the tears which you attempted to difguife by laughing, nor that I have perceived that you did not fqueeze my hand when I offered it to you fo cordially?"

" Don't

" Don't fpeak of it, deareft Count. I am, indeed, not well."

" Indeed not? And that malady attacks you in the very moment in which I feel myfelf well again the firft time?"

" Deareft, beft Count; for God's fake, don't be bitter. I cannot, I cannot bear it to day."

" Bitter!" he exclaimed, with a mien which was ten times more fo. " It is, indeed, the firft time to day that any perfon taxes me with it. I was not bitter while I was unfortunate; it muft therefore originate in my happinefs. " But," added he, in a foothing accent, " do you really think that I am fuch a bad and inattentive obferver, that I fhould not have feen at whom your tendereft and moft burning looks were directed?"

" Pray, tell me, at whom were they directed?"

" The former at my fair neighbour, and the latter at myfelf. The tears, that
ftarted

ftarted from your eyes, could not extinguifh their jealous fire."

"Jealous, did you fay? By heaven I do
not comprehend you."

"Alas! how much is my Carlos altered! Can that be *my* Carlos, whom I
doat upon, who was the tender partner of
my joys and forrows, my guardian genius,
the fharer of all my fecrets and my in-
moft thoughts, whom I looked upon as
my better half? I fcarcely can perfuade
myfelf that he is the fame perfon. By
his kind affiftance I have recovered from
a dangerous illnefs, and he does not re-
joice at his own work."

"Lewis, your reproaches are unjuft.
By the eternal God! I never have loved
you with a greater ardour than in that fatal moment. But you are not miftaken;
I am ill, very ill. I fcarcely know myfelf
again."

Here a torrent of tears relieved me at
once. My pulfe began to beat with uncommon violence, my whole frame was

convulfed; a feverifh tremor fhook all my
limbs, I never have experienced fimilar
fymptoms. All the agonizing feelings of
my ftraitened heart convulfively communicated themfelves, as it were, to every
part of my agitated frame. The Count
was almoft petrified at the fight of thefe
emotions, which thrilled me by fits, and
which I ftruggled in vain to overcome. I
wanted to fpeak; however, my teeth chat-
tered fo violently, that I could utter none
but inarticulate accents. I wanted to
fhake hands with him, but trembled fo
exceffively, that I miffed his. I wanted
to recline my head againft his bofom, and
relapfed half-fainting upon the fofa.

"What a myfterious incident!" he exclaimed ever and anon. "I çannot perfuade myfelf that you are really ill: or
fhall I fend for a phyfician?"

I begged him, in the greateft agony,
for a little water and wine; my mouth
being fo much parched that I fcarcely
could open my lips. He gave it me, and
I felt

felt myfelf refrefhed. He now feated himfelf upon the fofa, to wipe the cold fweat from my face with his handkerchief, entreating me, again and again, to com- pofe myfelf. " All will be well," he added. " You know how little I value my life, if I can be ufeful to you: fhould I, therefore, not willingly fhare my hap- pinefs with my dear Carlos?"

" Deareft Lewis!" I groaned, "rather a thoufand reproaches, than that heavenly goodnefs. Alas! I do not deferve it." So faying, I ftruggled to difengage myfelf in a fit of wild defpair from his embraces; however, he would not let me go.

" If *you* don't deferve that love, that tender kindnefs; who elfe can merit it?

" Tell me, O! tell me, my injured friend, do you really not hate a rival?"

" A rival! Is this the fatal fecret? Yes, Carlos, I confefs Caroline could make me happy, and obliterate the recollection of what I have fuffered. My paffion began as early as yours. It fways in my breaft

F 2                    equally

equally powerful as in your poor heart.
We have the fame right; but I muft tell
you, that I believe my hopes are better
founded than yours." I fhuddered violently. "However," he continued with
a deep groan, " you have nothing to fear;
I ceafe, from this moment, to be your
rival. I rather will renounce happinefs
for ever, than purchafe it at the expenfe
of your tranquillity and peace of mind.
Here is my hand; Caroline is yours. I
renounce all my claims to her heart, and
leave you at full liberty to gain it for
yourfelf." So faying, he fqueezed my
hand, and ftrained me tenderly to his bofom. How was it poffible I could have
expreffed the grateful feelings of my
heart? However, he was fatisfied with
himfelf and with my tears. Every noble,
generous deed produces its own reward.
Broken accents fpeak ftronger, and with
greater energy, than words; and amongft
all languages that of gratitude is the
moft monofyllabled.

He

He now left me to myself with his
ufual gentlenefs. His eyes were, indeed,
rather overcaft with a melancholy gloom,
and his brow was not cloudlefs; yet he
reftrained his grief at the facrifice he had
made, and fpared my feelings. But, alas!
what a dreadful night fucceeded that fatal
evening! my fever encreafed after the
Count's noble declaration, and the dawn
of morning found me abforpt in gloomy
reveries.

" This is then the fruit of thy fufferings,
thy travels, obfervations, and refolution?"
I faid to myfelf: " thy moft folemn vows,
and thy vaunted friendfhip are wrecked
upon a miferable paffion? How deeply
muft he defpife me! And has he not the
greateft reafon for it? Is he not greater
than I? Did he not tell me that Caroline
would render him happy for life, and reftore his long loft hilarity to him? He
never has enjoyed the blifs of love in its
fulleft extent, and I deprive him of it at
his commencement of a new life: I, who

F 3                                    am

am a voluptuary, a fpoiled fondling of
love, and have but lately wept at the early
tomb of an adored wife! Carlos, thou art
the meaneft wretch, and not deferving of
thy exiftence, if thou canft hefitate to return that facrifice."

It is incredible how much pain it coft
me to come to that refolution; a refolution that was too natural and juft than that
it ought to have appeared to me a facrifice. I began to meditate more ferioufly
upon it, and was aftonifhed at the unnatural ftate of my mind. The firft love
heats a blood that rolls through a youth-
ful, healthy frame; and the kindling fire
of fenfations that have juft unfolded themfelves, urges us beyond the limits of humanity; and yet my fenfes never have
been in fuch a tumultuous agitation; even
not when I firft met Elmira, animated
with a full fenfe of my pride, and confcious of fuccefs; nor when fhe dropt into
my trembling arms, encircling my neck
as my happy and blefling wife, and my
fenfes

fenfes were, for the firft time, inebriated,
on her bofom, with every rapture love is
capable to afford; nor was my blood
heated to a fimilar degree in Rofalia's
arms, who had taught me to empty the
cup of intoxicating fenfuality to the laft
drop. Maturer age alfo had contributed
to cool the heat of paffions; and Elmira's
modeft meeknefs, the dear cares of a tranquil domefticated life, unruffled by forrow, and flowing in a foft and gentle
ftream, had blunted the edge of my defires. What could, therefore, have deprived me of my fenfes in that moment;
what could have rendered me fo callous
againft the admonitions of a juft and
friendly heart; what could have been the
reafon of the vehement tempeft that agitated my whole nature?

While I was occupied with thefe and
fimilar reflections, which fucceeded each
other with an incomprehenfible impetuofity, the idea of my fingular fatalities in
Spain forced itfelf upon my foul. Don

Bernhard,

Bernhard, who conftantly frequented our houfe, though his character did not fuffer him to affift in all our banquets, happened that night to be of our party.   Count S\*\*\*\*\*\*i alfo was prefent; and both being in an uncommonly merry humour, they entertained the company with a relation of our little Bacchanals at Toledo.  The recollection of thofe merry fcenes reminded me, by a natural affociation of ideas, of the feparation of our fociety, and of the fate of its individual members.  I recollected that one was feduced by an Italian finger to abandon our cheerful circle; that a fecond was called away by family affairs; that a third was intoxicated by fomething mixed with his wine.   The latter idea made me ftart up with a loud fcream.   "Heavenly powers!" thought I, "fhould, perhaps, the unnatural ftate of my mind and body be the effect of a fimilar caufe?"   I hurried out of my bed. The dining room was feparated from my bed-chamber only by two apartments.  I

put

put a night-gown on, and went with the greateſt precaution thither, to aſcertain my ſuppoſition, if poſſible. The glaſſes were ſtill upon the table; the ſervants being uſed to remove every thing in the morning when the company ſtayed too long. The dawn of morning peeped already through the windows, and enabled me to diſcern every object without difficulty. I began to examine the glaſſes, but with very little hope of ſuccefs, as it alſo was poſſible that ſomething might have been mixed in my plate; nay, it even appeared to me to have been too hazardous to attempt mixing an inebriating drug with my wine or water; though I was ſo much abſorpt in thought, that I perhaps ſhould not have taken the leaſt notice of whole clouds of impurity in my glaſs. My apprehenſion ſoon was confirmed beyond contradiction; for I diſcovered in one of the glaſſes, ſtanding near the place where I had ſat, a whitiſh matter on the bottom, which undoubtedly was the re-

F 5                              mainder

mainder of what I inadvertently had fwal-
lowed.

The conclufions I deduced from that
difcovery were of a moft alarming nature.
It was evident that the agent of the au-
thors of that atrocious deed muft be one
of our fervants, and at the fame time have
few accomplices, or none at all. My fervants had, however, been employed very
little at table; thofe of the Count having
waited upon us from the moment he had
joined our company. I had, befides,
fufpected two of his people for fome
time; for thefe fellows were of fuch an
enormous and unnatural ftupidity, that I
could not conceive how the Count could
keep them in his fervice. Being, however, unwilling to throw an odium upon
an innocent perfon, I refolved to conceal
that incident and my fuppofitions from
my friend, and only to watch them with
the greateft vigilance. My blood being
ftill in a violent fermentation, I mixed
fome lemon juice with wine and water,

4                              which

which refreshed me more than I had expected. I could, indeed, not sleep; but
found myself a great deal better on the
subsequent morning.

### CHAPTER V.

THE Count, who came very early to
see how I did, found me pale and
languid. I entreated him to forget the
whole scene of last night, because I had
made the observation that I really was
very ill. He sent immediately for a phy-
sician, who shook his head, declaring my
illness to be a fever of a most dangerous
nature, and found it necessary to bleed
me. Yet I rose at ten o'clock, in health
and pretty good spirits, feeling no other
inconvenience than an ebullition in the
blood, and an unspeakable languour. I
was several times strongly tempted, in the
course of the day, to inform the Count of
my suspicions with regard to the affair of
last night; and had the best opportunity of

F 6                     doing

doing it at table, where I examined the wine, and every difh, with an unufual care, which occafioned him to afk me whether I was afraid to be poifoned by him? Yet that very queftion fealed my lips. His extraordinary agitation, and the ftruggle with his heart, which was not yet entirely decided, imparted to every thing he faid a certain bitternefs which he could not conceal, notwithftanding his endeavours to appear open and kind to me. Thus frail is the human heart. I faw, with fecret forrow, the diftrefs which the facrifice he had made me inflicted upon his agonized mind. I might have foothed his agony, if I had explained to him that my fingular behaviour on the preceding night had been owing rather to a difordered body than to a weaknefs of heart; however, his filent referve, and my being doubtful how he would re- ceive it, prevented me from coming to an explanation.

The

The only thing I did was to make obervations on myfelf; and the deeper I penetrated into the fecrets of my feelings, the more coldnefs to Caroline did I difcover in my heart. I was highly rejoiced at it, and yet apprehended that it was impoffible I loved her neverthelefs. I heated myfelf more violently in attempting to grow cooler, and fecretly afked myfelf, " Is it *poffible* you could love Caroline?" It fcarcely can be; and yet I apprehend it really is fo. She has, indeed, not gentlenefs and judgment enough, and alfo appears to have too much felf-will, as to be capable to facrifice much for her lover; however, fhe has a certain fpirit of converfation which charms me, and a natural infinuation that flatters felf-love, and muft render its object happy. But is all this worth facrificing a tried friend, whofe peace of mind appears to depend on her love? No, Carlos! be afhamed, and conquer a fatal paffion, that owes its exiftence merely to an unnatural ftate of thy body,

left

left thou becomeft the fport of others that have kindled it in thy heart, and ftrive to gain the applaufe of thy own underftanding, of the Count, thy friends." This foliloquy terminated in a folemn refolution to fhun Caroline as much as decency would permit, and I was determined to carry it that very day into execution. We were invited to an affembly, where we were fure to meet Caroline; my indifpofition affording me a natural pretext for ftaying at home, I refolved not to go. Not knowing how to amufe myfelf all the evening, I went to my clofet, and fearched for fome books. I carried at leaft half a dozen to my fofa, without being able to determine which I would read. I alfo had got fome mufic for my flute, and put a chair to the Piano forte. At length, I put a nightgown on, and ftretched myfelf upon the fofa, reading aloud, to filence the voice of my heart. Thus I was in an excellent way of fpending the evening in private, and to divert my mind, when fuddenly a

carriage

carriage ftopped at our houfe. I was violently frightened. " Good God!" faid I
to myfelf, " I hope I fhall not be difturbed
by vifitors!" fhut my eyes, and pretended
to be faft afleep.

Not two minutes were elapfed, when
my clofet-door was opened, and a perfon
entered. He approached the fofa foftly,
while I confulted with myfelf whether I
fhould not open my eyes a little to fee
who was fo kind to difturb my fweet repofe? It was the Count, and in full drefs.
" My God! in full drefs?" I exclaimed,
ftarting fuddenly up, and furveying him
with gazing looks.

" You play fine tricks, Marquis," he
faid coolly. " I really thought you was
faft afleep, and you ftart up at once as if
you were going to fly in my face!" So
faying, he put his fword on, which he carried in his hand, went to the looking
glafs, and examined his head-drefs.

Seeing that I ftill continued to look at
him without making the leaft attempt to
ftir,

ftir, he put his hat on, turned round, and
croffing his arms negligently, faid, " But
tell me, Marquis, what means that comedy you are acting there in your great
night-cap?"

" A comedy!" I replied, with looks of
aftonifhment.

" I think you have had fufficient time
to take your nap; though you have dined
to-day with an extraordinary appetite."

" You are miftaken, Count," I began
peevifhly: " I have had no appetite at
all."

I would have given any thing if I could
have provoked him to enter into a conteft
with me on that point; for I was determined to prove clearly that I never had
dined with lefs appetite. He went, however, to the window, without returning a
word, began to hum an air, looking into
the ftreet, and diffembled to be occupied
with fome ridiculous object. At length
he refumed, ftill looking out of the win-
                                    dow;

dow, "How long will you let your carriage wait at the door?"

"My carriage at the door! I don't
comprehend you. Have *you* ordered it?"

"Yes, I have; and it is your ftate-
carriage. Have you entirely forgot, that
I am the king of the feaft which we are to
have, and that the Minifter of H******
and the ****fh Ambaffador will be of the
party?"

"Pray tell me, dear Count," I replied,
"whether I am dreaming? for I affure
you, I know not a fyllable of it." (I
really had almoft entirely forgot it.)

"Have I ever feen the like?" he replied, turning round. "All the world
has been folemnly invited laft night. I
come to fetch you, and you are not dreffed.
Thefe are fine doings, indeed! I am fure
the card-tables will be occupied before
you are ready, and you may eafily conclude that I fhall play to-night?"

All my fine plans vanifhed in that moment : I faw nothing but the gay company,
dancing, playing and laughing.

"Well,

"Well, then, I muſt make haſte to dreſs," I replied mechanically, taking my cap off, and ringing for my valet. He came, and uſed ſuch expedition, that I was in my carriage a quarter of an hour after.

We came, indeed, too late; all the card-tables were already occupied; and Caroline having deſpaired to ſee the Count that night, had left the company to pay ſeveral viſits before ſupper. The Count was determined to play, and ſucceeded at length to collect a party. Being not diſpoſed to play at cards, I ſtole upon a balcony, which looked into a large yard covered with lofty trees, where I abandoned myſelf to pleaſing reveries. The deluſive duſk, the humming in the air, and the ominous ruſtling of the cooling breezes betwixt the trembling leaves, created ſweet ſenſations in my mind; and my imagination was agreeably occupied with forming pleaſing fancies, when the door behind me was opened at once. On

turning

turning round I beheld Caroline, who,
mean time, was returned, and had left the
apartment for reafons fimilar to mine.
She feemed not to have obferved me at
firft, being rather. ftartled when fhe faw
me. Yet fhe foon collected herfelf, falu-
ting me with her ufual good nature and
fimplicity, and inquiring how I did. I
began to tremble, and replied with vifible
confufion, and in broken accents.

She began to laugh, refuming gaily,
" I really think you have been fleeping,
Marquis, for your phrafes are uncommonly odd." I confeffed that I had
been dreaming, at leaft, and being afked
of whom, I replied, " of you, charming
Caroline."

Thus I opened a converfation on the
very fubject I had fo firmly determined to
avoid. She declined every thing I faid
with the gayeft humour, which impercep-
tibly led me to add a great deal more of
the fame nature. In fhort, our converfation grew very warm. She was violently
                                    agitated

agitated, notwithftanding her cheerful humour; and at length began repeatedly to
fpeak of the Count, pitying him with a
moft charming kindnefs for his palenefs
and melancholy, and even afked me
whether his heart was not the prey of fome
filent grief? She could have chofen neither
a fubject nor words that could have made
my blood ferment with greater violence.

When the air grew more chilling, fhe
told me fhe would go and fetch her fhawl,
and foon join me again. I offered to do
it for her; however, fhe infifted upon
going herfelf. I counted every minute;
but fhe did not return. Having waited
in vain above a quarter of an hour, I returned to the company. She fat by the
Count, looking in his cards, or rather
contemplating his beautiful countenance,
which exhibited ftriking marks of melancholy, and received additional charms by
the languid palenefs his illnefs had left
upon it. He never had appeared handfomer to me than that night. The fpeaking
language

language of his mien was indeed now and then interrupted by an indefcribable perplexity; however, the goodnefs of his heart continued to prevail in every feature of his benevolent countenance. His dark eyes, flafhing with a faint fire, fpoke powerfully to the heart; and the pale enamel of his lips refembled a rofe that firft begins to blufh.

Caroline was entirely abforpt in the contemplation of his affecting features; her face was the mirror of his, and repeated every mien of her melancholy neighbour by its movements. As foen as the Count perceived me by his fide, he endeavoured to involve me in a converfation with Caroline, who juft was ftarting up, exclaiming, "Good Heaven! I have forgot the Marquis, who waits for me on the balcony!" She was rejoiced to fee that I had joined the company, and drew her chair clofer to the Count.

The latter began, from that moment, to be entirely abfent, replying little, or
nothing

nothing at all, to her obfervations and queftions. This offended Caroline at laft, and fhe rofe fuddenly from the card-table, declaring that play did make people unaccountably infupportable. She then wifhed the Count, laughing, a good night; repairing to the oppofite fide of the apartment, where a forte piano ftood, and began to play.

Yet fhe could relifh nothing. I followed her like her fhade, taking up a violin to accompany her; felected fome of her favourite airs; but every thing was intolerable to her. She grew, at length, uncommonly fad and gloomy, reclining herfelf againft the back of her chair, fetched a deep figh, and fhut her eyes.

I did every thing in my power to amufe her; but nothing would do: fhe returned very fhort anfwers, and grew cooler every moment. She continued to keep up that humour till the gaming parties rofe; and being placed, at fupper, between the

Count

Count and myfelf, her cheerfulnefs foon
returned with additional luftre.

This charming change feemed, however, not to have the leaft effect on the
Count. He continued to be fad and
gloomy, however attentive and obliging
fhe was to him. She was indefatigable in
her exertions to roufe him from his melancholy ftupor, difplaying her wit and good
humour in the moft advantageous light;
but nothing would fucceed. The company was enchanted with her lively fallies
and acute remarks; the Count only was
dejected and abforpt in gloomy reveries.
He had formed his plan, and nothing
could tempt him to give up his refolution.
His pertinacy was fo firm, that neither
Heaven nor Hell would have been able to
draw him only a hair's breadth from his
courfe.

At length fhe grew tired of that frigi-
dity, and addreffed herfelf to me, to punifh him for his fullen referve, thinking,
perhaps, that jealoufy would effect what

love

love was not equal to perform. But she was miſtaken; for the Count grew more communicative, and I was as laconic as he had been. I was but too ſenſible of the real motive of the honour ſhe did me; my pride did not ſuffer me to avail myſelf of her favourable diſpoſition, and my cheerfulneſs was far from encreaſing. Thus the evening, for the pleaſures of which ſo many preparations had been made, was ſpent in a very irkſome and tedious manner.

From that time I ſaw Caroline almoſt every day; it was at leaſt not *my* fault if I did not. The Count's melancholy en-creaſed every day more viſibly; he fre-quently ſhut himſelf up in his clôſet, re-tired early from all companies, or ſtayed entirely at home. His friends aſcribed that love of ſolitude to the effects of his illneſs; and I confirmed their ſuppoſition. Every ſpark of generoſity ſeemed to be dead in my heart during that fatal period; I ſaw him ſtruggle againſt his paſſion with

an

an indifference that covers me with pungent fhame whenever I think of it; he
was a living picture of forrow, and I had
not even fo much feeling left to comfort
him. In fhort, I was fo completely, fo
thoroughly altered, that it is impoffible
my friends fhould not have noticed it.

The female heart is never entirely void
of vanity; and none that is not pre-occu-
pied, will be able to refift a firm and indefatigable exertion to gain upon it. I now
was frequently in private with Caroline,
and none of my other rivals was very
formidable. I really imagined to have
made fome impreffion upon her heart, and
that fhe had completely forgot the obftinate Count. I enjoyed that little, dubious
happinefs with a rapturous pleafure, when
an accident fuddenly overturned the airy
edifice of my vanity at once.

We met at the country feat of a friend
to celebrate a rural feaft. The fine feafon
was already on the verge; autumn had,
however, fufficient charms left to make us

VOL. III.          G          forget

forget the amufements of the town for a fhort time. The vintage was getting in, and that is the time when merriment and pleafure difplay themfelves in the moft natural and charming manner.

The neceffary preparations were made, at the country feat of my friend, folemnly to celebrate every day of that general re-joicing. The two moft virtuous girls of the village were publicly prefented in the church with a garland of white rofes, and received a very liberal dowry. Their beauty was, indeed, not equal to their virtue; yet they received that reward with fuch a grace, and fo much modeft inno-cence, that every one was convinced, be-yond contradiction, that they deferved having been felected from the reft of their fifters. This enchanting harmony between gracefulnefs and virtue is generally no where to be met with in that high degree as among the French peafantry.

No one could deny that all his fofter feelings were completely gratified among

that

that troop of amiable country girls who, during the fhort time of our ftay with them, never loft fight of us. Thefe remarks had a powerful influence on my fubfequent refolutions. All of us gentlemen were greater or leffer finners, and it afforded us the higheft pleafure to exchange the coquetry and art of our ladies with the fenfible and open fimplicity of thofe innocent children of nature. Joy and cheerful mirth animated, therefore, every one of us; and we found many little innocent means of gratifying our glowing humour, and the demands of a heated blood, without injuring the virtue of thofe innocent ruftics. Dancing and fongs, little feafts and proceffions, fire-works and comedies, followed each other in a pleafing fucceffion, were always different in their nature, and, neverthelefs, only parts of a well arranged whole.

Even the Count began to cheer up a little, yet without being able to take his ufual fhare in thefe amufements. Caroline

was

was ftill a little angry with him, or at leaft pretended to be fo; and being ufed to have always a declared lover, gave me the preference. I was obliged to fit always by her fide, to carry her gloves and her fan, and to follow her every where as her efquire. Even when fomebody talked to me at a fmall diftance from her, fhe inquired, with the greateft fimplicity, " where may the Marquis be?" This induced me to flatter myfelf to be fecretly beloved by her, though fhe never fuffered me to fpeak of my paffion. She neither acted the prude, nor was referved, but behaved like an offended wife that is going to lofe her hufband, and importuned already with propofals of a fecond marriage. The Count foon obferved that fhe feemed to be very partial to me, and frequently fqueezed my hand by ftealth with averted looks. Yet my proud heart foon conceived a prefumption upon her favour, which unexpectedly made me fenfible of my miftake.

One

One afternoon fhe roved with me thro'
the garden, playing numberlefs little
pranks. She was more immoderately
merry than I ever had feen her before, and
her amorous gambols fired me to a degree
of which I never thought myfelf fufceptible. She was, befides, dreffed with uncommon elegance and tafte. Her fine
fhape, the activity of her limbs, the pli-
ancy of every part of her graceful form,
the luxuriant growth of her curling hair,
which wantonly overfhaded her forehead
and bofom, and her eafy, cheerful gait,
made her refemble the Goddefs of Mirth.
I was intoxicated by the fight of her un-
prefuming charms, and enchanted by the
jovial roguery of her fparkling eyes.

Being, at length, exhaufted by her
playfome gambols, we feated ourfelves
upon the fwelling turf, where it was overfhaded by a tuft of myrtles. She broke
off fome of the depending twigs, and began to throw them at me. I had juft
picked up two, and was going to fling

G 3                                        them

them at her in return, when she suddenly
averted her face from me towards a walk
covered with lofty trees.   I turned round,
and beheld the Count coming slowly towards the place where we were sitting.
He was alone, and so profoundly absorpt
in thought, that he did not see us.   His
arms were crossed, his head depended
upon his bosom, his eyes were half shut,
and he seemed to be entirely unconscious
of the objects around him.   He made
now and then motions, as if he conversed
with some person, dropt one of his hands,
covering with the other a part of his
face.

Caroline suddenly grew serious; I
wanted to continue our frolicsome sport,
but she paid no attention to me, replying
to all my questions nothing but, " The
poor Count! how melancholy he is!"
" The poor Count!" I repeated with
great emotion; and one of her sweet looks
thanked me for my concern.

When

When he came nearer, without feeing us, I called to him. He awoke from his gloomy reverie a little frightened; yet he had too much power over his countenance as not to exhilarate it immediately; and he always grew extravagantly merry, whenever he changed from a melancholy mood to cheerfulnefs; which now alfo was the cafe. Yet Caroline could not be deceived by his unnatural jocundity; her countenance affumed an uncommon ferious afpect, which impelled him to ufe ftill greater efforts to cheer her up. I feconded him faithfully; and when nothing would fucceed, we grew, at laft, fo exceffively merry, that fhe offered to rife, and to leave us.

" I perceive, beautiful Caroline," he now began, " that one of us is difagreeable to you, and I fear I am that *one*."

Although he faid this in a laughing accent, yet Caroline returned neither a word, nor even a look; remaining quietly on her feat, and playing with her fan.

G 4 " No,

"No, no!" said I, "You are miftaken, dear Count; I am that perfon." I directed a fcrutinizing look at her while I uttered thefe words; but fhe ftill continued to be taciturn.

"You probably think fo," the Count refumed, "becaufe fhe is fo ferious ever fince an unfortunate accident has made me interrupt your converfation?"

"I don't like to enter into a conteft with you; but let us make an experiment. That proud goddefs may decide herfelf. Kneel down, and take this myrtle fprig." He kneeled, laughing, down, and took the myrtle in his hand.

"Now, fair Caroline," I began in a folemn accent, turning to her, "it is your turn to choofe. Here you fee two lovers kneeling before you, who adore you with equal tendernefs, who would facrifice their life with pleafure to fave yours, but rather will devote it to your happinefs. Either offers you a myrtle fprig, accept that of him whom you prefer to the other."

I could

I could not help thinking that it was
cruel to treat the poor Count thus: however, the prefent opportunity feemed to
offer me that little triumph in fuch a natural manner, that I could not refift the
temptation of enjoying it. My poor
neighbour trembled, and was in a violent
agitation, while I anticipated my victory
with a fmiling countenance. Caroline,
however, inftead of treating the matter as
a frolic, as I had expected, rofe with dignity, and in a very folemn manner, which
excited our aftonifhment; but no fooner
had fhe furveyed us with a dubious look,
than fhe loft all prefence of mind. Her
face was alternately overfpread with a deep
crimfon hue and a deadly palenefs; her
bofom heaved with greater violence, and
fhe breathed louder, covering her countenance repeatedly with her hand, and difplaying an uncommon emotion. After a
few feconds, fhe recovered the dominion
over herfelf, darting an unfpeakable tender look at the Count, who ftared at her

G 5          like

like a ſtatue, and another leſs ſignificant
one at myſelf, ſnatched with vehemence
the myrtle ſprig from my friend's hand,
averting her face, and ſaid, in a trembling accent, "I thank you, dear Count."

It is a kind of miracle that I did not
loſe the uſe of my ſenſes on the ſpot. It
rather ſeemed as if I had received a thou-
ſand eyes more, to ſee more plainly what
now enſued. The Count was almoſt
frantic with rapture, forgetting every
thing, the world and myſelf, and ſtrain-
ing the trembling girl to his boſom. At
firſt, ſhe only ſuffered his careſſes and
kiſſes, but ſoon returned them with equal
fervour. Tender looks, and voluptuous
ſighs, were mutually exchanged, and the
glowing fire of love burned on their crim-
ſoned lips. They were infolded in tender
embraces, while I continued to kneel
before them in a kind of ſenſeleſs ſtupor.

The Count obſerved, at length, my
forlorn ſituation, and raiſed me with a
grateful look. " My Caroline," ſaid he

to

to the fweet girl, " let my deareft friend have a fhare in your affection." So faying, he preffed me to Caroline's bofom. Heaven was in his looks; he believed to have regained every thing while he could ftrain the dear object of his love and the friend of his heart to his heaving bofom.

" Yes, Marquis," Caroline began, " I fhould have preferred you to all the world, if I had not known the Count. Be my friend, as you have been that of my Lewis, and you always will find my heart open, kind, and affectionately difpofed to you."

I was feized with ftunning ftupor, and incapable of returning an anfwer; I even could not evince my gratitude by a mute fign. I bent my weeping eyes upon the hand which fhe extended to me, and felt it burn more violently than my face. This was the only fenfation of which I was confcious. My heart ceafed almoft to beat, and a chilling tremour thrilled my frame, but was foon fucceeded by a con-

vulfive

vulfive heat. My breaſt heaved violently, and yet I had it not in my power to un-burthen it by a ſingle ſigh.

The Count embraced me, ſqueezing my hand. "You know, my dear Carlos," he added, "that my rapture is not unal-loyed with pungent grief."

Caroline now raiſed me up, putting my hand between her arm, while the Count took hold of me on the other ſide. They ſpoke little; however, their tender looks conveyed comfort to my poor heart. I was ſcarcely conſcious of being led by them.

"This then is the conſequence of thy adventurous undertaking," ſaid I to my-ſelf in the evening, when I was alone in my apartment: "fate has puniſhed thee as thou didſt deſerve. Yet it is fortu-nate enough that that deciſion, that the certainty of thy fate, has cooled thy fooliſh preſumption, and that thou haſt a greater ſhare of pride than of any other paſſion."

I cannot

I cannot but confefs that my pride only
faved me, my paffion being not ftrong
enough to refift it. I never had, till then,
loved without hope; and even Caroline
had opened a favourable profpect to me
by her innocent fportivenefs. The firft
blow my humbled vanity received was
dreadful enough, yet it foon recovered
from that unexpected fhock, and rendered
me eafy. I fhould have been blind, if I
could have overlooked the Count's fuperior
merits, his enchanting form, his gay and
even temper, and his fenfible heart, which
was ever ready to make the greateft facri-
fices to the objects of its love. Yet no
one will expect that I fhould have been
able to witnefs the felicity of the two
lovers with tranquillity. I refolved, therefore, patiently to keep them company,
while they fhould remain in the country,
and then to repair to fome other part of
the world; a refolution, the firft part of
which I performed more faithfully than I
had reafon to expect. I took fuch a tranquil,

quil, but lefs cheerful, fhare in all their
amufements, deceived myfelf fo much by
my equanimity, and forced myfelf to fuch
an impofing unconcern, that the ferenity
of the Count, who firmly believed that
I foon would be cured entirely, vifibly
encreafed, and grew every day more natural.

But how great was his aftonifhment
when I entered his apartment, a few days
after our return to Paris, and informed
him that I was going to leave him for a
fhort time. He fcarcely could believe
that I was ferious: I told him, however,
that he was miftaken if he imagined my
heart was as cheerful as my countenance.
I alledged fuch ftrong and reafonable mo-
tives for a tour through France, and a vifit
to a little eftate I poffeffed in Provence,
that he approved my plan at laft, though
it was very vifible that it gave him pain
to part with me even for a fhort time.
We found, however, fome comfort in the
hope of a fpeedy cure of my mental
                                    difeafe,

difeafe, and of my fubfequent return. I
had, befides, found out the moft amiable
travelling companion I could wifh for:
this was Count S******i, who was in a
fituation fimilar to mine, and fincerely rejoiced at my propofal. The Count and
myfelf being now completely reconciled,
we embraced each other with an affectio-
nate heart and weeping eyes. He offered
to fpend the night with me, and to accompany me the fubfequent morning a
few leagues. Wifhing, however, that my
journey fhould be looked upon merely as
a pleafure excurfion, I defired that the
farewell-fcene fhould be as fhort as poffible. Having, therefore, fettled the manner in which our correfpondence was to
be carried on, I difengaged myfelf from
his embraces, and fpent the night in private in my apartment, giving audience
to my thoughts, and preparing for my
departure.

S******i and myfelf had agreed not to
render our journey tirefome, by taking

too much care of our convenience on the road. We provided ourfelves with good horfes, and very little baggage; and were attended only by two fervants. Being thus accoutred, we began our excurfion, independent on the rudenefs of the poft-mafters, who are of one caft all over the world. As for my companion, I had not the leaft apprehenfion of falling out with him, for he was good-nature itfelf. I called at his apartments with the firft dawn of the morning; we mounted our horfes, and the Count wifhed us a pleafant journey from the balcony.

## CHAPTER VI.

S\*\*\*\*\*\*i and I left Paris with light hearts, and cheerfully anticipated the pleafures which awaited us. Our hilarity encreafed with every mile that carried us farther from the refidence of every terref-trial happinefs. We did not regret it in the leaft; and were entirely occupied with the

the ferenity of the fky, with our plans,
and the good-natured cheerfulnefs of the
country people. Berry lay before us, and
promifed to afford us ample fcope for obfervations and amufement. Autumn was
on the verge, and the wind whiftled more
chilly and bleak through the fading leaves:
this is, however, the very feafon that
agrees beft with a certain wearinefs of foul.
My companion was, befides, a man that
would have been capable of foothing the
acuteft forrows; for a moft infinuating
gentlenefs animated every word of his,
and he took the warmeft intereft in the
leaft trifle that concerned the heart. The
objects that prefented themfelves to his
eyes, made him completely forget all his
cares; his exuberant imagination was fufficiently purified by the trial of early difappointments and fufferings; and his hilarity of mind reflected a cheerful light on
every object that prefented itfelf to his
eyes. His heart was the amicable abode
of tender fenfibility; and he was too good-
                                        natured

natured to confine his friendfhip to an individual fellow-creature, cherifhing the
whole human race with undivided affection.

We travelled for fome time without
meeting with any remarkable incident,
accelerating our courfe whenever we
thought proper, and ftopping at every
place which promifed to afford us pleafure.
Count S******i being difpofed by nature,
and I by my fate, by philofophy and ftern
neceffity, to find every where fcope for
amufement, we met at all places where we
ftopped a kind reception, and people with
whom we could converfe.  Nothing is
more ridiculous than to travel for the fake
of amufement and improvement, and at
the fame time to pay a nice attention to
one's rank.  I have known very few ram-
blers who travelled with that intention,
that did not difplay more or lefs of that
foolifh pomp.  A traveller never ought to
expect real pleafure and benefit from his
rambles, if he is not initiated in the great

art

art of being a peafant amongft country
people, an artift amongft artifts, and a
merchant amongft merchants.

I have never known a man who poffeffed
the different qualities and perfections
which compofe that art in a more extenfive
compafs than S******i; his temper, which
breathed nothing but cheerfulnefs and af-
fability, appropinquating him to every
open phyfiognomy. He fpoke the language of all ranks, knew all their prejudices, their favourite ideas, and peculiar
expreffions. He could affume almoft any
fhape; and no one could refift his manner,
which fpoke a language that is generally
underftood, the language of the heart.
My rambling life, and the frequent changes
of my fituation, had taught me alfo a
little knowledge of man; but whenever I
was near him, I was but too fenfible that
I was obliged to exert all my attention, if
I would fpoil nothing. He ftole almoft
irrefiftibly upon every heart; and fcarcely
a quarter of an hour elapfed before he was
the

the idol of people who faw him the firft time. There was no reft in the houfe before our horfes were watered and baited, and our dinner or fupper got ready. All was in a buftle: fix feet were in motion as foon as one fignified a wifh; they affembled cheerfully around us; fpoke freely, and without difguife, of every thing. The prettieft girls were felected to dance with us, or offered themfelves voluntarily with the moft amiable fimplicity and innocence. Wherever we fhewed ourfelves, we beheld joy and good will depicted on every countenance; and were happy even amid the fmoke of feveral dozens of tobacco pipes. If we ftayed more than one day at a village, fome little feaft was generally given on our account; the beft bottle of wine was fetched out of the cellar; the young girls of the place were affembled; and thefe poor people, who only wanted a pretext for being merry, were rendered happy for feveral hours by the fhare we took in their amufements.

S******i,

S******i, in return, flighted neither their difhes, nor their offers, nor their fociety; he ate and drank with every one what was offered to him; danced as well with the ugly as with the handfome villagers without difcrimination; fpoke and laughed with every one at whatever they chofe; and frequently played a ballad on the guittar, or related his travels. Such a filence did then prevail around us, that one could have heard the falling of a feather. the company fat gaping on the benches, and hardly dared to fetch breath before the tale was concluded; the confequence of which was, that thefe poor people parted with us with weeping eyes, or ran a quarter of a mile after us, on our departure.

At Blois we happened to meet the Duke of B******, and gave occafion to that proud Briton, who thought to carry every thing by the weight of his purfe, to make a very mortifying experience. Having arrived early in the morning, we determined

mined to take a ride after dinner, and to
furvey the environs of the town. The
Duke arrived, not long before our return,
with two coaches, two valets, feven or
eight giant-like fervants, and two led-
horfes. The landlady, who was preparing
our fupper, hefitated a while whether fhe
fhould admit the proud Peer with his numerous retinue, notwithftanding the difplay of his guineas, as fhe could forefee
that he would give her fo much trouble
that fhe fhould not be able to enjoy our
fociety. At length fhe gave the keys of
the apartments to the waiter, and ordered
him to fhew the Duke up. The purfe-
proud Nobleman being ufed to be received
with the greateft refpect at the inns, was
aftonifhed to fee himfelf ufhered in by the
waiter, the landlady being juft occupied
to prepare a rice cream, which Count
S******i had ordered; and the landlord
gone in queft of a bottle of *Vin de la Cote*,
which my friend had wifhed to have.

The

The Duke took, however, poſſeſſion of his apartments, and ſuddenly a dreadful noiſe aroſe in the yard. Our two ſervants had been watering their horſes, while the Duke's people had quartered theirs in our ſtable, which appeared to them to be more commodious, and better than the reſt. Our truſty eſquires were aſtoniſhed. to find, on their return, the receptacle of their beaſts occupied by new inhabitants; and having not the leaſt inclination to be diſlodged, Antonio diſmounted ſilently, with all poſſible Spaniſh grandezza, led the intruders into the yard, and put his horſes in poſſeſſion of their former ſtation, in preſence of all the ſervants, who were ſtruck with aſtoniſhment on ſeeing the beaſts of an Engliſh Peer treated thus diſreſpectfully, and diſlodged by two miſerable hacks, as they were pleaſed to call them.

Their indignation ſoon broke out into dreadful curſes; and they aſked Alfonſo, with kindling rage, how he dared to re-

move

move the horfes of an Englifh Lord. A
loud laugh was the only anfwer my fervant
returned. He locked the ftable, and
having put the key coolly into his pocket,
was going to ftep into the houfe. The
Duke's fervants feeing themfelves treated
with fo much difrefpect, grew furious;
and the conteft foon became fo clamorous
and warm, that the Peer, hearing the
voices of his people, opened the window
of his bed-chamber, and defired to know
the caufe of their quarrel. Being informed
of Alfonfo's temerity, he ordered him, in
a domineering accent, to deliver up the
key, and to put his horfes into another
ftable. The fervants exulted already at
their fuppofed victory; but Alfonfo
pleaded, with the greateft civility, his
prior claims to the ftable, and declared
that he rather would lofe his life than give
up the key. The Peer being highly exafperated at his obftinacy, ordered his fervants to take it from him by force; and
his people having only waited for the fignal

nal of attack, fell furioufly upon poor
Alfonfo. The honeft fellow being affailed
by feven ftrong and lufty men, faw no
other expedient of faving the key, than
to throw it into an open window, which
went into the kitchen where the landlady was bufily occupied with the Count's
rice cream.

She had been amufed already for fome
time by the fcene which was acting under
her window, and fecretly applauded Alfonfo's fpirited conduct. He poffeffed,
like my friend S******i, a fecret charm to
ingratiate himfelf with all the landladies
we met with on our journey; and our
hoftefs no fooner faw him fling the key
into the kitchen, than fhe took it for a
fignal to come to his affiftance, and inftantly armed herfelf with her largeft
fkimmer to terminate the conteft. She was
firmly refolved to hit a found blow at the
lufty fellow who had feized her dear Alfonfo
by the collar, when the landlord appeared
on the field of battle, carrying the bottle

VOL. III.          H                  with

the coftly wine, which he had got at laft, after numberlefs fruitlefs inquiries, triumphantly under his arm. He was inftantly informed of the caufe of the conteft in a moft clamorous manner, and haftened with his yoke-mate to poor Alfonfo's relief.

The Duke's fervants being more defirous to get the key into their poffeffion than to vent their vengeance againft my man, had already unhanded him, when they came up with them, without having done him any other harm than beating a hole into his head as large as a fhilling. It may eafily be conceived what a terrible clamour our landlady raifed when fhe beheld the broken head of her favourite. "Good god! what will the dear gentlemen fay on their return!" fhe exclaimed ever and anon. "Holy Peter! how they will be enraged!" Mean time, one of the Duke's fervants attempted to get into the houfe to fetch the key, which fhe no fooner perceived, than fhe hit him fuch a

dreadful

dreadful blow with her culinary weapon in the face, that the poor fellow ftaggered back with a roaring yell.

The Duke now ordered his people to defift from all further contention; for although he was an Englifhman, yet he did not poffefs a large fhare of that undaunted courage for which his countrymen are renowned; and having learnt, by the exclamation of the landlady, that Alfonfo had a mafter, which till then had not come into his Lordfhip's mind, he thought it prudent to proceed with lefs violence. The hoftefs did, however, no fooner efpy him at the window, than fhe let loofe the reins of her tongue, thinking him to be the chief caufe of that incident. She read fuch a lecture to the Englifhman on the impudence of his people, as he probably never had heard before. Her hufband too, who was not in the habit of agreeing with his loving fpoufe, was of the fame opinion with her, declaring that the ftable could be parted with for *no price*.

H 2                              The

The Duke thinking the honour of his
nation was at ftake, looked upon this Phi-
lippic as a challenge to throw fome guineas
out of the window: however, that indeli-
cate expedient only ferved to exafperate the
hoft more violently; yet he contented himfelf with kicking them indignantly afide,
and proceeded to the Duke's apartment,
to remonftrate with him on his conduct.
The latter was, by our hoft's obftinacy,
inflamed with fuch an eagernefs of getting
poffeffion of the ftable, that he offered a
confiderable fum of money; and at laft
threatened to quit the houfe immediately.
But neither the one nor the other made
the leaft impreffion upon the headftrong
landlord; and the Peer was, at length,
obliged to drop the conteft, becaufe he knew
that he could not get poft-horfes before
the next day, and apprehended that he
fhould find no accommodation in another
inn.

The hoft was juft going to quit the
apartment, when the Duke perceived the
bottle

bottle he carried under his arm. He inquired after the name of the wine, and
it happened unfortunately to be his Lordfhip's favourite liqour. He began, therefore, to make new offers; but the hoft
was equally inexorable: nay, he was even
fo malicious as to extoll the delicioufnefs
of the wine to the fkies; adding, that he
had found it extremely difficult to get a
bottle of it, and that he would take no
price for it. The Duke inquiring after the
reafon of fuch ftrange behaviour, the hoft,
who was impatient to difplay his attachment to the Count, enumerated our merits
in a moft hyperbolical manner, and laid a
particular ftrefs on the defcription he was
pleafed to give of our noble fpirit and
bravery. "Thefe two gentlemen do, indeed, travel in a fimple and unexpenfive
manner," he concluded: "however, I
will be hanged if they are not two foreign
princes who travel incognito." Thefe
words had the defired effect on the Duke:
he now began ferioufly to think that his

H 3                                    heat

heat had mifled him to commit a very foolifh action, and afked the landlord, with vifible perplexity, how he thought Alfonfo could be indemnified beft. The landlord fhook his head, declaring, that he was afraid it could not be done by money; and an attempt which the Duke made to that purpofe confirmed his fuppo-fition. We returned from our excurfion in the moment the landlord had finifhed his parley. The Duke was at the window, and feemed to be aftonifhed at the majef-tic appearance of the Count, whofe un-commonly beautiful horfe was prancing in the yard. The noble animal was of a high mettle, and gave his rider an oppor-tunity of difplaying his fkill in horfeman-fhip. Mean-while the landlady came running out of the houfe to feize the reins of the horfe, thinking the Count was in danger; and Alfonfo, whofe head was bound up, was clofe at her heels. We difmounted; and feeing a number of

ftrange

ftrange fervants in the houfe, could partly
guefs at the affair.

Having patiently liftened to the minute
account of our kind landlady, we found
that it was of a complexion which made
it neceffary we fhould wait upon his Lordfhip immediately. He received us with
an incredible perplexity, which he ftrove
to conceal as much as poffible. My ad-
drefs was very fhort; and, without men-
tioning our names, or inquiring for his, I
afked him what fort of fatisfaction he
meant to give to my fervant for the ill
treatment of which he had been the principal caufe? He ftarted fome difficulties;
but at length grew more reafonable, begging my pardon; and we parted with mutual civility.

We frequently met with fimilar inftances;
for the vanity of men is greater than
their defire for gain. We had entirely
divefted ourfelves of our rank and dignity;
and without abandoning, only for a moment, that elegance of deportment which

H 4 always

always diftinguifhes a man of noble birth
and a good education, flattered the paffions and prejudices of every one. *Little*
friends ought not to be flighted, as well as
petty enemies; and we frequently received
the greateft fervices from people of whom
we had not expected the fmalleft kindnefs.
The innkeepers and their people rivalled
every where to treat us as well as poffible:
the lefs we required, and the more fatisfied we feemed to be with what they
could give us, the more did they exert
themfelves to render us every kind of fervice, and to anticipate our wifhes; the
confequence of which was, that we never
had any reafon to complain of the infolence and the impofition of the landlords;
and we were convinced, by repeated experience, that travellers generally have
to accufe no perfon but themfelves if
they are not well treated by the innkeepers.

One evening we had already left Chartres
far behind us, and approached a village,
whofe folitary, but romantic, fituation
promifed

promifed us, if not a convenient, at leaft
an agreeable, accommodation for the
night. We had made it a rule to decline
as much as poffible from the high road,
bending our courfe generally towards a village on the top of a rifing eminence,
or fecluded from the reft of the world in
a deep valley. There nature was purer,
happinefs more artlefs; the inhabitants
were handfomer and more cordial; and
the reception was kinder than in the neighbourhood of more cultivated manners.

   And why did we travel? Was a ftatif-
tic fpeculation, or the examination of the
different degrees of morality, or of churches
and fteeples, or of bridges and edifices;
were the fine arts, or any thing of that kind,
the objects of our peregrination? Certainly not. If one is defirous to travel
for that purpofe, one muft not ftop long
at Paris, where fpeculation finds fuch
an ample fcope, and where the fineft
products of art, and the objects of the
moft luxuriant phyfical and moral re-
finement are fo numerous, that a refi-
                 H 5                        dence

dence of a twelvemonth at that gay capital blunts the senses and the mind almost
entirely; takes away every relish for such
objects, at least for a confiderable time;
and excites an irrefiftible defire to fly from
that fatiguing buftle, and to reft the weary
mind, and the fatiated fenfes, on the bofom of pure and artlefs nature. This
was our aim, and conftituted our fole
pleafure.

The hamlet, which now hailed our eyes,
feemed to confift only of a few houfes;
and reclined fo artfully againft the fteep
declivity of a rock, that it was almoft
perpendicularly fufpended over a preci-
pice. The eminence terminated, on both
fides, in a plain, which was covered with
a number of a fertile hillocks, and exhibited a variegated mixture of garden
ground, meadows, and wood. Art feemed
to have joined with nature to mix the co-
lours in the moft pleafing manner.

The fenfations of the traveller chiefly
depend upon trifles. Nothing, therefore,
produces

produces a more picturesque effect than
the rising smoke of a solitary chimney
concealed between a cluster of trees.
Hunger, fatigue, and curiosity, lead us
to form an idea conformable to the dispo-
sition of our imagination, or to the wants
of the moment of the scene which is before us: we anticipate the enjoyment of
every thing we expect to find, mould the
faces into the form in which we wish to
meet them, and reduce the circumstances
to the shape that would be the most
convenient to us.   Nothing is truer than
that not the enjoyment makes us happy,
but its approach.


## CHAPTER VII.

IT was Sunday when we arrived at the
hamlet.   All the inhabitants were affembled beneath a large wallnut-tree, and
their joy was rather clamorous. One muft
have feen French peasants, to form an
adequate idea of the fcene which pre-

fented itfelf to our eyes. The opprefled
and the poor generally abandon themfelves
to exceffes whenever they can catch a moment of liberty, tranquillity, and fuper-
fluity; and the human heart, which much
fooner is urged from one extreme to the
other than cooled to moderation, deftroys,
without hefitation, a part of future pleafure, while it abandons itfelf to the rapid
torrent of prefent gratification.

The young people danced, and the
girls were adorned with autumnal flowers.
Some branches compofed charming huts,
where we received refrefhments fpread on
benches. . Their whole orcheftra confifted
of a fingle fiddle, a tambourine, a fife,
and a clarinet: however, the female
dancers moved with fo much agility and
natural grace, that the eyes were indemnified for what the ears miffed. We paffed
the dancers in a hard trot, being impatient
to arrive at the inn which was on the other
fide of the hamlet. The curiofity of feeing us ride by, put a momentary ftop to
the

the dance and the mufic, which began
again, as foon as we were paft, with the
fame unconftraint as if no obfervers were
near. Our drefs was foon changed: the
Count put on a flight white night-gown:
I followed his example; and thus accoutred, we went in our flippers to the dancing place, attended by our landlady, who
gazed with vifible delight at my friend's
elegant form and graceful carriage. I
alfo could not help making the fame remarks I read on her countenance. He
had the appearance of a king in difguife.
His foft blue eye glittered with that tranquil majefty, which peacefully raifed itfelf above the preffure of forrows; his
looks fpoke the fweet language of general
benevolence; and his colour, which commonly was rather pale, had been animated,
by exercife and good humour, with a rofy
hue, which was charmingly fet off by the
diforder of his brown hair. The noble
grace of his gait, and of his whole carriage, eafily could tempt one to believe that
he

he was an inhabitant of Heaven's realms, who had left his celeftial abode to blefs the mortal race.

When we approached the dancing place, we obferved fome motions among the merry company. They feemed to confult how we fhould be received: however, we joined them with as much eafe as if we had lived many years amongft them; faluted every one, and fhook hands with thofe who were moft contiguous to us. The little confufion our arrival had caufed was thereby inftantly difpelled; and when we told them that we wifhed to take a cordial fhare in their joy, they raifed a loud fhout of fatisfaction. We were led to the beft feat: the oldeft of the happy circle offered us wine, figs, almonds, and grapes; and the mufic and dancing began anew.

Having refrefhed ourfelves fufficiently, we did not hefitate to mix with the dancers. The Count chofe a partner; and I alfo had no difficulty to find one for myfelf.

felf. The vanity which our charmers felt
at that preferment, foon raifed them above
the referve which is natural to the female
fex; and the blufhing, innocent damfels
joined their hands cheerfully with ours.
The Count's partner was a tall, jolly bru-
nette; and I was coupled to a little, languifhing girl. The former was by far too
fiery for the character of her partner, and
the latter too gentle for me; yet the beauty
of their form, the fimple, animated and
well conducted dance, which unfolded
their charms in the moft advantageous
manner, foon made us forget the recipro-
cal contraft of our difpofitions.

*Annette,* the partner of my friend, had
the fineft fhape I ever beheld ; a fmall,
pale face, full and rofy lips, and a round
voluptuous chin. Her black eyes fpoke,
or, at leaft, would not fpeak, much that
evening; for I remarked afterwards that
they could be pretty eloquent. She fported
with the innocent careffes of the poor
Count, who feemed to be enchanted with
her,

her, though he was not wont to brook female feverity. He was probably fo pliant at firft merely for the fake of amufement, but at laft his fentiments took a more ferious turn.

*Lucy*, my fair partner, was Annette's younger fifter, and quite the reverfe of her; a little, languifhing, puny being, of uncommonly fine limbs, and a moft pliant make. Her foft eye, overfhaded with long, brown eye-lafhes, feemed, indeed, not to be an entire ftranger to roguifh coquetry; yet it difplayed more modeft goodnefs than wantonnefs. It burned with a wifh, with a fecret defire, for a certain fomething, which fhe, perhaps, had no clear notion of, or at leaft, feemed never to have found as yet. Her bofom fpoke the fame language, as well as the blufhes of her dimpled cheeks, when I preffed her little charming hand. Her feelings certainly were ftrong, and fhe only was at a lofs how to exprefs them. She had too little energy of body and of mind, and

for

for that reafon, feemed not to be fufceptible of a higher culture, as fhe indeed was
fenfible of the impreffion of the prefent
moment, but did not retain it long.

· We fpent the evening in congenial, artlefs pleafure, frequently changed our partners, according to the eftablifhed cuftom,
but always returned to thofe our good fortune had beftowed upon us at firft. The
Count's charming impartiality forfook
him at once, and I did not hefitate to
imitate his example, impelled, as it were,
by an unaccountable fecret enchantment.
If one has, or only imagines to have, received fome pleafing fenfual gratification,
the firft impreffion, the firft tafte, always
predominates ftrongly among thofe that
fucceed it. There were at leaft twenty
lovely figures among thefe little fweet
country girls, that were prettier and more
charming than our partners; however, we
were almoft entirely infenfible to their
beauty. . The fecret impulfe that urged us
to return to our charmers, cannot be called
                                        love,

love, it rather was a ftrange fort of a namelefs defire. The fhape and the manners of the lovers infpired the reft with a jealoufy which rather feemed to be owing to offended vanity than to a particular inclination towards us. The general good underftanding was foon interrupted; the favoured fair ones indulged themfelves with feveral little liberties; the reft did not care to difguife their indignation; and, befides, we were not the fole lovers of our partners. It was owing merely to the fuppofed fuperiority of our rank, which was confirmed by the noble carriage of the Count, that this general difatisfaction did not break out: however, the filence which began to prevail around us rapidly encreafed every moment; the general inebriation of pleafure gradually vanifhed as one little troop feparated itfelf by degrees from the reft; and thofe who were infpired with fimilar fentiments, retired at fome diftance in fmall groups, taking no farther fhare in our diverfion.

Our

Our ladies, too, were fenfible of our mif-
conduct, and grew gradually more referved; and we now were the only perfons
that did not obferve it.

I was at length reminded of it by Alfonfo, who, all the evening, had been a
filent obferver of our behaviour, without
taking the leaft fhare in our diverfions. I
imparted his remarks fecretly to the
Count, and our eyes were opened at once.
We now beheld ourfelves and our partners entirely deferted by the company,
and the reft difperfed in feveral groups.
However, we neglected to make a
proper ufe of that difcovery, being diverted by the jealoufy of the company;
and, inftead of behaving with more cir-
cumfpection, encreafed our careffes and
our attention to our partners, which vexed
their lovers in fuch a degree, that they
drew nearer with glowing faces, and with
looks which plainly told us that it was
high time to difcontinue our ungentle-
man-like fport.

Night

Night was, fortunately, fetting in. The
families broke up, and went to their refpective homes, probably very little edi-
fied by the conclufion of their rural ball
and our conduct. Annette and Lucy alfo
were impatient to go home: we offered
them our arms, and attended them to
their houfe, amid the pretty audible hiffes
of thofe that had ftaid behind.

There are fituations in human life in
which we really feem to be controuled by
fome magic charm, of which the events
of that evening were a fpeaking inftance.
All thefe humiliating confequences of our
conduct, the cold civility of the old people, the fcornful looks of the girls, the
wry faces of the young men, and even the
referve and growing coldnefs of our
charmers, were not fufficient to make us
fenfible of our foolifh imprudence. The
landlord and his dame, who, fome hours
before, had received us with fo much
kindnefs, and attended us, had alfo
changed their looks very much on our return:

turn: even our fervants convinced us, by their geftures, that they did not much ad-mire our prudence. Every thing was, befides, in a confufion to which we were not accuftomed, and which we had not yet experienced on our excurfion. The horfes had bad ftabling, and not yet got their fodder: no fupper was to be feen; and having, at length, put the people of the houfe in motion, our meal turned out fo meagre and miferable, that we went to bed with empty ftomachs. We now be-gan, almoft at one time, to rail at the people of the houfe, inftead of looking for the caufe of our difappointment in our conduct; and were fo much infatuated as to curfe and to threaten our hoft, to quarrel with our fervants, to beat cats and dogs, and feveral times were very near falling out with each other before we went to our apartment.

On coming to our bed-chamber, an additional caufe of diffatisfaction threw itfelf in our way; only one fpare bed being, unfortunately,

unfortunately, in the houfe. This inconvenience would, indeed, not have given us
the leaft uneafinefs at any other time,
either of us taking it rather as a favour to
be fuffered to fleep on a chair if the bed
happened to be too fmall to contain both.
But now, neither would refign the bed to
the other; and, after a long and warm
contention, we fqueezed ourfelves at length
into the narrow compafs of our uncom-
fortable couch. Yet we were incapable
of getting a wink of fleep, tofling ourfelves from one fide to the other, and mur-
muring alternately at our miferable fituation. We had the additional misfortune
to be almoft fuffocated by an intenfe heat,
which, at length, drove me out of the
bed. I began to walk up and down in
the room, and the Count foon followed
my example, ftepping to the window, and
inhaling the frefh night air.

"What the D——l does that mean?"
he exclaimed at once, ftarting fuddenly
back. "Look, Carlos, what a numerous
                                    crowd

crowd gathers under our window." I
haftened to him, and actually beheld about
twenty young people before our door, but
could difcern nothing elfe, the night being very dark. We now began to guefs
and to conjecture what could be the meaning of that affemblage, and naturally concluded that it muft have fome connection
with the incidents at the dancing place.
I was violently enraged at the infolence
of our nocturnal vifitors; but Count
S******i, whofe good humour returned at
once, began to laugh. This inflamed me
ftill more vehemently; and, inftead of
being pacified by his unconcern, I apprehended fome danger. I fetched, therefore, our piftols; and having made every
preparation for a vigorous defence, was
going to awake our fervants. Count
S******i was, however, more prudent
than myfelf, and ftopping me at the door,
with a loud laugh, faid, " Don't put
yourfelf into a paffion; I will lay any
thing that their whole drift is nothing but
a miferable

a miferable frolic. Don't fpoil the pleafure of thefe poor fellows, but rather let
us divert ourfelves at their expenfe."

The event proved that he was not miftaken; for we were, after a few minutes,
regaled with an excellent ferenade, whofe
harmony foon informed us of its meaning.
The effect this charming concert had on
my rifibility was fo powerful, that I could
not have refifted an immoderate fit of
laughter if it had coft me my life. The
mufic could certainly not be called a fym-
phony; however, fo much is certain, that
the moft horrid notes were borrowed from
all inftruments to produce a kind of cho-
rus. As much as I could diftinguifh,
fome horns were the principal inftruments;
and it may eafily be conceived how charmingly they were blown: a fiddle, with only
one ftring, two or three rattles, a da-
maged trumpet, fome little drums, and
three or four kettles, accompanied the
performers who played thofe agreeable
inftruments; and fome fmall French
whiftles,

whiftles, which are ufed to call the flocks
together, in the neighbourhood of which
one is in danger to lofe one's hearing for
ever, completed, by their fhrill notes, the
harmony of the whole. Several other inftruments I did not know; however, the
whole concert was of fuch a nature, that
it would have been able to refufcitate the
dead, and to reduce nervous people to the
brink of the grave.

We were amufed for fome time: however, the Count took, at length, a pocket
piftol out, and having extracted the ball,
fired it over their heads. It caufed a louder
report than I had expected, and the mufic
was filenced in an inftant. The young
gentlemen, who had not conceived the
moft diftant idea of the ferious confequences which might attend their frolic,
did not think proper to finifh their ferenade, and left us fuddenly to our reflections.

The Count continued to laugh immoderately, and I was infected by his merry

humour. "It would be excellent sport," he exclaimed, "if we could dispossess these fellows of their pretty little girls. I would give any thing." I was entirely of his opinion, protesting that nothing could be more pleasant. Our vexation at our disastrous circumstances had divided us, and the resentment these very circumstances created united us again. We now consulted about the means of effecting our purpose, and soon hit upon measures which promised us success.

The execution of our plan was more successful at first than we had expected, as the final issue of it was more unfortunate and mortifying than we ever could have imagined. The young people had again a dance the next evening; and we prepared the whole hamlet, during the day, for our behaviour on that occasion. We were as gentle as doves, and seemed to be good-nature and condescension itself; wandered through the hamlet, paying very little attention to the girls; joked with the

young

young men, and were ferious in the company of the old ones; flattered the mothers, and treated the daughters with cold civility. When we entered a houfe, we were received with frigid referve and four looks, but pleafure and good-will beamed in the eye of every inmate when we left it: our falutes were returned with cordiality; every one was charmed with our conduct; and every thing changed in our favour. Yet we were too much exafperated as to drop our defign, and impatient to be revenged for the treatment we experienced laft night.

Our behaviour in the evening was alfo entirely changed. We betrayed not the leaft defire to mix with the dancers, but affociated with the old peafants, difcourfed of the vintage, made our obfervations on the wind and the clouds, prefaged the weather, and pretended to know the meaning of the croaking of the frogs. The gaping peafants were aftonifhed at the ftriking change of our behaviour, and

liftened

liftened fo eagerly to our difcourfes, that
here and there a pipe dropt on the ground.
Every recollection of the events of the
preceding night feemed to be obliterated,
and the liftening circle, that ftood around
us, encreafed with every minute. The
Count fang and played on the guittar; and
I relieved him at intervals by the relation
of wonderful incidents, and of ludicrous
anecdotes. The dance ceafed, and the
girls too affembled around us; however,
we took little notice of them.

*Annette* and *Lucy* were ftruck with aftonifhment at our behaviour with regard
to themfelves. They were drefled in their
beft apparel, and their difappointment
was legibly written on their countenance.
Annette affected to be entirely indifferent
to the Count's inattention to her perfon,
and ftrove to be extravagantly merry:
Lucy, on the contrary, fcarcely could retain her tears; and the more her fifter
exerted herfelf to make the company burft
with laughter, the more frequently did fhe
take

take her pocket handkerchief out to wipe her eyes.

Not the leaft of thefe circumftances efcaped our obfervation, and our looks frequently met thofe of our offended fair ones; yet nothing was able to make the fmalleft impreffion on our obdurate hearts: they were obliged to go home unattended; and we returned to the inn, accompanied by almoft all the inhabitants of the hamlet, who feemed to adore us.

No fooner were we left to ourfelves, than we broke out in a fit of laughter, congratulating ourfelves mutually on our excellent talents for hypocrify, deceit, and courtly difguife, as well as on the impreffion we flattered ourfelves to have made on the hearts of our charmers. We really had appeared more to our advantage to day than the evening before in our night gowns and flippers. The Count was dreffed in his uniform, which, indeed, did not become him half fo well as his white night gown: the buttons of his mi-

I 3                              litary

litary drefs were, however, fo bright, and
the rich embroidery of his coat was fo re-
fulgent, that every 'look was attracted by
the fplendor of his external appearance,
which-received additional charms by the
bloom of health blufhing on his cheeks,
and the fparkling luftre of his eyes. Love,
unblended with any kind of ambition,
is, befides, rather unnatural; and the
latter is frequently the father of the
former.

The next morning we converfed, in the
prefence of our landlord, on the happinefs a conftant refidence at fuch a charming fpot, and with fuch good-natured
people, muft afford. Our hoft now affumed a very fly look, affuring us that he
was not fo ignorant of the ftate of our
hearts as we perhaps imagined, and declaring that he would do as much as lay
in his power to put us in poffeffion of the
two girls whom we had found fo charming
the firft evening, provided we were willing
to marry them. He added, they were
the

the richeſt in the village, each of them
poſſeſſing a large farm of her own; and
we might be ſure of ſucceſs, if we would
avail ourſelves of his interpoſition, as he
was their uncle and godfather, and had a
great influence on the family.

I feigned to be aſtoniſhed at his ſaga-
city, replying, in my and in the Count's
name, that he had completely gueſſed the
real ſtate of our hearts, and that we ſhould
avail ourſelves of his kind offer as ſoon as
we perceived that the girls were favourably
inclined to us; mean-while we wiſhed to
hire a ſmall farm for ſome time.

We were fortunate enough to have the
choice of two, and hired that which required the leaſt labour; becauſe neither
the Count nor myſelf was over fond of too
much exertion, but knew how to ſet a
proper value on eaſe and convenience. It
was, however, requiſite we ſhould act the
part of farmers in the higheſt perfection
poſſible; and while we exerted ourſelves
to the utmoſt of our power to do honour

I 4                              to

to our new ftation, we actually incurred
the danger of being rufticated. I do not
know what opinion S******i entertained
of me with regard to that point; however,
his behaviour gave me juft reafon for
thinking thus of him. He could eafily
accommodate himfelf to almoft any fituation; and its character, which he appro-
priated to himfelf, foon became completely
natural to him. He preffed, as it were,
the effence out of all fcenes and circumftances of human life, and always found
fomething agreeable in the enjoyment
thereof. Ere long, his borrowed character
grew habitual with him; and he never
left his affumed manners before they re-
linquifhed him, or a new fituation required it.

I, on the contrary, did not fo eafily and
fo perfectly catch the fpirit of a character.
My difpofition of mind, which always
leads me back to the time paft, and renders the gratification the prefent moment
affords agreeable to me only as far as it
harmonizes

harmonizes with the images of my fancy,
embellifhed by the diftance of time, ren--
ders every fituation very foon irkfome to
me. Being averfe to yield to the alluring
charms of novelty, it gains fome gratification only by a long continued ftudy of
an object, and therefore approaches it
only flowly. But not one moment of human life is alike to the other; the events
we experience, and our notions, are eter-
nally fluctuating and changing; and the
moment in which I begin to grow fufficiently intimate with the exifting circumftances, is generally the period in which I
commence a new exiftence.

I acted, therefore, my part a good deal
worfe than the Count, who found it very
convenient to attend perfonally the pafture
of his flock; to adorn his hat and bofom
with ribbons and flowers; to dine beneath
a fpreading lime-tree, to blow a melting
air on the flute, or to compofe the moft
heart-breaking paftorals. It was, however, very unfortunate, that the fine feafon

I 5                                    was

was already paft; a flower was a rarity;
not one human being heard his plaintive
ftrains; and his verfes, which favoured
already of the winter, were generally
obliged to be thawed before the kitchen
fire along with their author, before they
were palatable; and were loft to the world,
and to immortality, becaufe no perfon
heard them but myfelf.

I took care of the internal economy of
our houfe; and, with the two fervants,
fed and milked the cows, and prepared
our meals. We three feemed to prefer
having a good joint of meat in the pot,
and a profpect of a fubftantial dinner, to
hunting for rhimes all the day long.
When the Count returned, and had pro-
perly arranged his ideas, he began to fpeak
with enthufiafm of the graces of poetry,
and of the celeftial, immortal fire of love.
His character had received fome fatal luna-
tic fpots from the reading of fome German
novels, and his fancies more frequently
breathed an odour of the grave than of found
fenfe.

fenfe. Heaven knows how it came that I
never was more materially difpofed than
at that period. I rather endured than coincided with his fine fentiments. If the
morning was ferene and pure, my feelings
were neither more nor lefs elevated than
thofe of the brute creation: when the
moon fhone bright, I could, indeed, re-
joice for half an hour at her filvery orb;
and a fweet melancholy, now and then,
ftole upon me; but, inftead of fhedding
fentimental tears, I took my gun or a net,
to fhoot a good bird or to catch fifh, affifted by her deceiving flight.

Being occupied and diverted by labour,
allured by no temptation, and fafe from
the corruptive poifon of idlenefs, my
heart feemed, at that time, to be as
healthy as my body. I can, indeed, not
deny that a certain lady of the capital of
France attended me fometimes in my little
occupations. She was, however, rather
gay and cheerful than gloomy and fad;
and, what was ftill more agreeable, came

L 6                 always

always in the company of a third perfon.
I thought very little of *Lucy* and her
whole tribe, but neverthelefs lent always,
after our meals, a patient ear to the
Count's amorous complaints, laughing in-
wardly at my friend, that he was fuch a
fool to fall thus violently in love.

As for our fociable life, it was regulated
in the following manner: In the week
every one was hard at work; for our hamlet was poor, and the inhabitants lived
upon the fcanty produce of their agricul-
ture, pafturage, vintage, and the making
of wooden fpoons. The time lying very
heavy upon my hands for want of fociety,
I employed my idle hours in the fabrica-
tion of the latter article, and improved fo
rapidly, that I foon was famed in the
whole hamlet for making the fineft wooden
fpoons. I had learned, in Germany, to
make bafkets, and now exercifed that art
alfo in great perfection. When I was fitting in the yard bending ofiers, then it
grew frequently lighter in my foul than at
any

any other time; I fmiled cheerfully at the
time paft, and was highly fenfible that nothing in the world fmooths the path
through life fo much as conftant occupation
and labour, which leaves no fcope for idle
fpeculation.

This predominant propenfity for activity, which, being intimately connected
with my nature, has frequently urged me,
in the courfe of my life, to commit the
moft adventurous follies, made me ftiffer,
and lefs fociable, than the Count was rendered by his poetical idlenefs. When he
returned from his paftoral world with his
cows and his fheep, he ufually was in fuch
a good humour, and his imagination was
fo bright and active, that every object prefented itfelf to him in a rofy-coloured
light; and his rapture knew no bounds
when he had fucceeded in being happily
delivered of fome fine poem, or had feen
his fhepherdefs, and received a kind look
from her. He almoft choaked me with
his enthufiaftic extravagancies; and when
                                  I fhewed

ᴇ

I shewed him a fine spoon I had made, or
a neat basket which I had finished, he left
me suddenly, ran through the whole hamlet, knocked at every window where he
saw a light, disturbed our neighbours in
their sleep, tired them with his unseason-
able discourses, found every where wit,
found sense, simplicity, and honesty, ho-
noured, at last, his mistress with a ballad
of the time of Henry IV. or of Lewis XI.
and persuaded her he had composed it for
her that very day.   When I returned with
my gun or net, I generally went for him
to her house, or delivered him from the
teeth of some mastiffs, who could not
conceive what business he could have in
the street at so late an hour.

He made, however, excellent progress
in his courtship.   Annette had already
confessed to him that she loved and preferred him to the rest of her lovers; and
nothing but the marriage ceremony de-
barred him from the completion of his
happiness.   This was, however, a point
with

with refpect to which the Count poffeffed
as little of the fpirit of cofmopolitifm as
myfelf; for he profeffed the juft principle,
that, as a man of the world could not be
certain to be happy *with* his lady, one
ought to take care to get fomething along
with her, that at leaft would make fome
atonement for difappointments which
might happen, and fweeten the bitternefs
which oftentimes is mixed in the cup of
matrimonial blifs.

I was not fo fucoefsful in my love, for
which I probably had to thank nobody
but myfelf; for while the fiery fair ones
*feem* to make great pretenfions, thofe of a
gentler difpofition *actually* demand a great
deal. They do not eafily forget little neg-
lects, refent every fault one commits, and
reflect at home on what one imagines to
have been forgot in a moment. A great
propenfity for an eafy and quiet life has
always been a predominant ftricture of my
character, notwithftanding its reftleffnefs;
and my gallantry to the ladies was feldom
carried

carried to a very high degree, if my heart did not, of its own accord, urge me to tender thofe flattering affiduities that commonly are held to be the criterion of a fervent love.

Lucy profited, therefore, very little by my paffion. I did, indeed, occafionally play a little air on the flute under her window at night, or danced twice with her on a Sunday, when the other damfels had that honour only once; or if I could get a nofegay without much difficulty, I prefented it to her, entwined with a blue ribbon, in a bafket of my own workmanfhip. I alfo told her fometimes, in the moft elegant manner, if fhe was alone, and feemed to wifh for it, that fhe was as beautiful as an angel, that I adored her, and that it depended entirely upon her to be beloved by me for ever. If I was in an uncommonly good humour, I even ventured to fteal a kifs, and to repeat the fweet theft if fhe was angry at my boldnefs. This was, however, all I did for her. My rufticated

phlegm

phlegm did not fuffer me to venture farther. The fervour of the firft evening
had been damped by the ferenade; and I
fhould have been vexed to death at our
foolifh frolic, if I had not been diverted
by the cares attending my culinary and
domeftic employment.

It was, at bottom, nothing but kindnefs for the Count that prompted me to
await patiently the conclufion of our
whimfical farce; for love appeared to me,
at that time, to be nothing elfe but an occupation fit only for idle people. The
work I had on my hand quickened the
circulation of my blood, enlivened my
ideas, and rendered them more healthy,
which enabled me to improve confiderably, in that fituation, in the true philofophy of life.

Unfortunately, our pleafure did not
laft much longer. The hamlet was too
far remote from the high-road than that
its inhabitants could have attained a great
knowledge of the gallantry of the nation.
It

It was, therefore, the cuftom with them to marry firft, and then to commence to make love. The fervants had, befides, not been over-careful to conceal our rank; and we had rendered ourfelves very fufpected the firft night. The father of the two girls being heartily tired of the trouble of guarding their virgin treafure, and feeing their former lovers relinquifh them, applied frankly to the Count, defiring him to declare whether we would marry his girls or not. S******i wanted to pacify him by an evafive anfwer and vague excufes: however, the farmer declared he perceived the drift of our courtfhip, and knew very well that it was impoffible a ferious alliance between ourfelves and his daughters could ever take place; defiring him, at the fame time, in the politeft manner, never to enter his houfe again, nor to appear under the window, if he did not choofe to expofe himfelf to difagreeable accidents. My poor friend really was feized with defpair; for although he

- had

had no mind to marry, yet he was violently
in love with his charmer. He now told
the fields his forrows, and the echo repeated his defponding complaints. The
moon and the ftars were moft ruefully in-
voked to witnefs his tears and his defpair.
His amorous fury and grief were, however,
only poetical. He did, indeed, rove the
fields, abfcond himfelf in the moft folitary receffes of the wood, gaze wildly at
the waterfalls, and conjure the chilling
autumnal gales, which only the abfence of
all feeling could miftake for Zephyrs, to
waft his fighs and amorous complaints to
his cruel Phyllis.

I was not difpleafed at that unfavourable
turn of our affairs: and if the girls only
had been a little more of our party, this
would have afforded the fineft opportunity
for adventures. My healthy blood fpoke of
nothing but of murder and elopement.
Oppofition made me enterprifing; and I
could have torn our faithlefs inamoratas
from the bofom of their parents, and carried

them

them to the moft diftant parts of the globe.
But the misfortune was, that the girls
were not at all difpofed to elope; and I
laughed, at laft, at myfelf and the Count,
and refolved to attempt his converfion to
found fenfe.

I never performed a good work with
lefs difficulty; for he foon began to laugh
at himfelf and me. He coincided with
my humour, and we began publicly to
act the furious lovers. We quarrelled
every day with the father of the girls, and
not a night paffed without a ferenade under their window. The whole hamlet
was put into an inteftine commotion, and
divided in different parties. A deputa-
tion appeared, at length, at our farm,
and requefted us refpectfully to depart in
peace. This was juft what we wanted: we
yielded, therefore, generoufly to their
humble requeft, fettled our affairs, fold
our cows and fheep, paid our rent, and departed laughing, highly elated by the ridiculous termination of our frolic.

CHAPTER

## CHAPTER VIII.

I FORBEAR troubling my readers with an enumeration of the changes that little adventure, which, at bottom, was a mere nothing, produced in my character. They will be perceived, without my affiftance, in the fequel of my hiftory. The chief effect it produced was a growing coldnefs to Caroline. A fluctuation with regard to this point too, in which I had, till then, difplayed a firmnefs that reflected honour on my character; a fudden breaking from a kind of mental fleep, a ftrong internal ebullition, fleeting fenfations, hazarded prefenfions, a high degree of activity, and a fubfequent ftate of apathy, made me dream, then urged me again to hunt eagerly after peace and happinefs, and, when I imagined to have found them, to throw them away fuddenly. The enthufiafm arifing from a quicker circulation of the blood was paft;

and

and I now commence that period in which
an unfatisfied internal fenfe, an ardent defire for activity, begins to ftir, and at
length relapfes again into its former dormant ftate.

The gay periods of my life are now on
the verge, and my career grows more ferious. The wanton fports of an exuberant imagination are on the decline; and
the reader foon will behold the birth of a
new love, great and facred, glowing and
powerful, without any nourifhment for the
fenfes, new-moulding my whole character, difpelling its fhades, raifing the luftre
of its brighter parts, artlefs and omnipo-
tent. The vicious fpirit of an abominable
confederation purifies itfelf in its genial
fire; and moments are dawning in which
the veil of mortality drops before me,
and my fpirit foars beyond the confines of
humanity.

I cannot conceive how it came that,
after this incident, I found my difpofition
not quite fo cloudlefs as before, every gra-

2                          tification

tification being blended with a greater degree of care, and joy and gaiety lefs benevolently fmiling upon me. I relapfed
into ferious contemplations; and although
I was neither diffatisfied nor melancholy,
yet I could, notwithftanding the circum-
fpection with which I continually watched
over myfelf, never recover that cheerful
ftation from which that ludicrous adventure had expelled me. I was conftantly
obliged to fpur myfelf to activity; and I
am almoft inclined to believe that my
tafte, and my notions of tranquillity and
happinefs, were entirely changed.

I was, as it were, gradually prepared
for the impending period of my adventures: a ferious, but inviting, fhade
fpread itfelf over every object that came
in my way; and I felt as if I returned
from the ferene luxury of an exuberant
and gay landfcape, to the melancholy,
fweet night of a fragrant grove carpeted
over with aromatic flowers, and animated
with the plaintive notes of the folitary
                                nightingale.

nightingale. Former scenes of joy, and the heart-expanding retrospect of the past events of my life, now reprefented themfelves to my mind, and abforpt me in fweet reveries. I enjoyed neither the effence nor the external of thofe events, but only the fentiments and notions which they produced and nurtured in my foul.

The Count either was infected by me; or a different caufe had, perhaps, produced the fame effect. He fpoke lefs, and was more frequently abforpt in ferious reflections. Formerly he had now and then, and always with fuccefs, trufted to hazard; but now he confulted carefully with himfelf before he attempted any thing, and the confequence conftantly turned out unfavourable. It was very natural that he was not difpofed to afcribe the caufe of this phenomenon to himfelf, for he found it without difficulty in the capricious humour of fickle Fortune. He was fullen and gloomy whenever he could find an excufe for being fo; and my altered looks

always

always afforded him a palpable plea for relapfing in that cheerlefs humour.

Do the events of human life really follow a pre-delineated trait, or does chance fometimes produce oddly united circumftances? Our minds were, indeed, now and then, cheered by lucid and pleafing intervals. Our good humour frequently made ample amends, in an hour, for what we had neglected in the courfe of feveral days, when we were refrefhed by a found fleep, if the morning was clear, not too cold, and neither wind nor fnow troubled us on the road, which was lefs frequently the cafe the nearer we approached the fouth of France. The moft important morning of my life was alfo the fineft I recollect ever to have feen; my mind too partook of the ferenity of the fky.

January was already on the verge; and the winter having been as mild as fpring, fummer feemed to be drawing near. The almond trees were already high in blof-

VOL. III. K fom,

fom, and the fhrubs began to be invefted with a leafy verdure. The olive woods, with their unfading green, embofomed already every where germinating wheat-fields; and the lark, the harmonious herald of the morn, ftrained its warbling throat to welcome the approach of the fine feafon. The returning fpring carries along with it a genial warmth, which dif-fufes itfelf through body and mind; every gentle gale breathes an animating fpirit; the myftic humming in the air, and the almoft vifible growth of the budding plants, produces a fymbol of a cheerful refurrection. And when we behold again, for the firft time, a flower, and the fun-beams gleam through the young leaves, our heart is thrilled with a heavenly rap-ture, and our language is too poor to do juftice to our feelings.

A fecret pulfation in my blood, a myftic unaccountable preffure againft my panting heart, a fudden ftop of the gentle ftream of my thoughts, frequently difturbed the

peace

peace of my mind on that heavenly morning. Every thing around me feemed to
be animated with namelefs beings; the
myftic founds which pervaded the foreft,
the fluctuating of the fun-beams in the
rifing vapours, the fparkling dew-drops
gliding from one leaf upon the other, the
current ftreams of vernal warmth, formed
in my bufy imagination a fmiling picture,
without colour, without a diftinct contour
and centre. The whole was attended
with a certain obfcure prefenfion, with an
ominous, though unintelligible, meaning;
and fome myftic certainty lurked in my
foul, without my daring to confide in it
the reality of its exiftence. The beauti-
fulleft landfcape hailed our enraptured
looks: yet its beauty rather confifted in a
fecret charm which my foul, unknowing-
ly and fecretly, imparted to it, than in the
fweet variegated mixture of its parts. On
our right a beautiful country feat ftretched
extenfive gardens and pleafure grounds
over the contiguous chain of hills: fmiling,

K 2                    picturefque

picturefque groups of trees, and little neat cottages, defcended from the declivity into the vale. A rofy-coloured morning va-pour was ftill fweetly blended with the bluifh colorit of the back ground, and, where it was lefs intenfe, exhibited to our view fome part of a village, the lower part of a rock, or trees whofe tops towered above the vaporous ocean. The caftle, whofe fcite we alfo could defcry only par-tially, was not far diftant; and the morn-ing fun reflected with radiant fplendor from its flaming windows. It was, with its light-green trees, fairy-like fufpended in the mifty back-ground.

We arrived at length at the park; and one of our fervants (I do not recollect whether it was Alfonfo, or that of the Count) began to repeat to us the informa-tion he had gathered from the landlord in whofe houfe we had flept the preceding night, with regard to the Lord of the Manor. He was a mifanthrope, fecluded from the world by misfortunes, who edu-cated

cated here a daughter famous for her uncommon beauty. Adelheid, Baronnefs
of V\*\*\*\*\*\*l, was the brighteft ornament
and the admiration of the whole province.
She lived. however, a folitary life, having
no intercourfe with her neighbours; few
had feen, and a ftill fmaller number ever
fpoken to her.

This information agitated me in a fingular manner. "V\*\*\*\*\*\*l!" I exclaimed:
"have you heard right?"

"I cannot be miftaken, My Lord,"
he replied.

"The name is very familiar to me:
fhould he, perhaps, be the father of
V\*\*\*\*\*\*l?"

"Whofe life you faved at G\*\*\*\*\*\*,"
Antonio interrupted me.

"The very perfon," I refumed. "I
now recollect that he frequently has converfed with me of his father and fifter;
and I am certain he was a native of this
province."

K 3                                    In

In that moment I rejoiced at my good
deed. When I refided at G******, that
young man fell into the river. He could not
fwim, and was in danger of being drowned. I inftantly plunged into the water,
and was fo fortunate to fave his life. This
was, indeed, no heroic action, as I was a
good fwimmer; and it had entirely flipt
my memory; but now I recollected it with
pleafure.

I took; from that moment, a warmer
intereft in every object I beheld. The
wall was low, and I could furvey all the
walks. " Perhaps (thought I) thou wilt
meet young V******l in the bofom of his
family, happy and animated with friendfhip for thee."

I was profoundly abforpt in the pleafing
fenfations this idea created in my heart,
when Count S******i fuddenly exclaimed,
" Stop! Marquis: for Heaven's fake ftop!
You will inftantly drop from your horfe.
Don't you perceive that your horfe's girth
has got loofe?"

I ftopped

I ftopped to alight, the fervants not being within call. However, he dif-mounted, exclaiming, with his amiable kindnefs, "Keep your feat: my faddle, too, wants to be tied fafter." While he was employed to bind the girth fafter, I made fome motions to make it eafier to him, and in the fame moment my looks catched a white object in the park. My heart began violently to palpitate; a cold tremour pervaded my limbs; and I fcarcely was capable to keep myfelf in the faddle.

A female being, of an heavenly form, walked in the park, within a fmall diftance from the wall. She carried a book in one hand, and with the other fcreened her face againft the dazzling rays of the fun, reflecting, as it feemed, upon what fhe had read. A little green ftraw-hat, fixed with a white ribbon beneath her chin, overfhaded her long auburn treffes, which depended in beautiful ringlets upon her gir-dle: the morning breezes fported with her

K 4                               white

white gown, which was tied round the
waift with a green fafh: her uplifted hand
was whiter than the muflin from which it
ftole forth, and the rofeate fmile of health
was diffufed over her countenance. Her
gown being unfortunately caught by a
brier, fhe was obliged to remove her hand
from her eyes to difentangle it; and having
extricated her garment, her black eyes
met me by accident. She ftarted a little
when fhe faw us fo contiguous to her; a
deeper hue blufhed over her delicate face,
and fhe caft her eyes fuddenly to the
ground, as if in fearch for fomething.
My horfe, whom I inadvertently had
pricked with my fpurs, began fuddenly to
bound; the Count called to me to be on
my guard. She looked once more at me,
growing as pale as afhes, and quickened
her paces. I pacified my horfe; and
while fhe turned round a corner into another walk, fhe directed her beautiful eyes
again at me; and in that moment the
Count too obferved her, exclaiming,
                              " Eternal

"Eternal God!" It is impoffible to fay
more to the praife of a beautiful object
than thefe two words, the aftonifhment and
the features of my friend expreffed; and
yet it was by far too little. My heart
was thrilled with unutterable fenfations,
and an unknown fomething pervaded my
whole frame.

I could not conceal the ftate of my
heart, which expreffed itfelf legibly on
my countenance. The Count obferved
me awhile feized with fpeechlefs aftonifhment, and at laft broke out in the words,
" Poor G******!" He perceived the
growing paffion; and knowing that my
temper was too irritable than that I ever
could be fortunate in love, wifhed to be
able to deftroy my paffion in the bud.
" But how fhall I accomplifh this?" he
faid to himfelf. " It is impoffible her
foul fhould entirely anfwer her external
appearance. There is no poffibility to
prevent my poor friend from getting acquainted with her; I will, therefore, affift
K 5                            him;

him; and if he fees himfelf difappointed
in his fanguine expectations, the cure of
his paffion will foon be effected."

He told me, therefore, laughing, " I
perceive, Marquis, I fhall have an opportunity to act here the fame part you un-
dertook from friendfhip for me in our
winter quarters."      But apprehending his
untimely joke would offend me, he added,
in a foothing accent, " yet I hope, Carlos,
you will repofe confidence in me!"      He
accompanied thefe words with a hearty
fqueeze of his hand, which I returned
cordially.. Mean while we were arrived
at the village, and difmounted at the inn.
While I retired to a private apartment, to
give audience to my thoughts, the Count
mixed with the people of the houfe, and
having made feveral inquiries concerning
the Lord of the Manor, wrote the following note in my name, and fent it to the
caftle.

" The Marquis of G****** has had the
honour to be intimately acquainted with a
Mr.

Mr. de V\*\*\*\*\*\*l. Having great reaſon to believe that Baron de V\*\*\*\*\*\*l is the happy parent of that excellent young man, he begs leave to pay his reſpects to the father of his friend."

His ambaſſador returned in the courſe of a few minutes with one of the Baron's ſervants, and a formal invitation for my-ſelf and the Count. Our horſes were in-ſtantly taken out of the ſtable, and our ſervants deſired to bring them with our portmanteaus to the caſtle. "You muſt be very intimate with the Baron, or ſtrongly recommended to him," the land-lord ſaid to the Count, ſhaking his head.

The latter now came to my apartment, and finding me on the bed, abſorpt in a profound reverie, ſaid, "Will you not get up, Marquis? The Baron," he added coolly, "has juſt ſent us an invitation to come to the caſtle."

" How! the Baron, did you ſay?" I exclaimed.

K 6                    " Yes,

"Yes, yes, the Baron," he replied, ᵂ
fmiling, and related his artifice to me. I
preffed him to my bofom, tranfported
with rapturous joy, and we went to the
caftle, but Heaven knows with what an
anxiety on my part. My knees trembled,
and my heart palpitated violently. I was
obliged to take hold of my friend's arm,
left our conductor fhould perceive my
emotion by my gait. Whenever I looked
at the windows of the caftle, and faw the
curtains move, I was violently agitated,
my tongue trembled, and I could fcarcely
fpeak intelligibly. The attention of fome
fervants, who ftood at the gate, opening
the folding doors on our approach, made
the blood rufh into my face; and I now
began firft to make the obfervation that
our drefs was very indifferent; for, to
confefs the truth, I had nothing on but a
fimple green hunting coat, and my hair
was in the greateft diforder. I could not
help communicating thefe remarks, in a
whifper, to the Count. However, he
                                fmiled,

smiled, replying, in German, " What a vanity! I affure you, you never have looked better!" We entered the caftle, at length. A man, who appeared to be the butler, welcomed us with refpectful politenefs, informing us that he had orders to fhew us to the drawing room, till his mafter was dreffed. We were conducted to a fpacious apartment, decorated with a number of portraits and other pictures. The fervant having withdrawn, we began to examine the pictures. They were, probably, family pieces. I did, indeed, gaze at every one of them, but without the leaft attention, my mind being differently occupied. I admired, at length, even the frames of fome, declaring the carving to be excellent, when the Count quickly replied, " Dear Marquis, if you are fuch an admirer of frames, then come, and look at this: I am fure you never faw a finer one." I went to the other fide of the apartment where he was, and he exclaimed, again and again, " Is it poffible
any

any thing could be.more elegant than this
frame?" "You are miftaken, dear Count;
for the garland of yon picture is much
more beautiful and elegant." "I am of a
contrary opinion," he replied, laughing:
"this is of a much better workmanfhip.
Upon my honour the picture does not deferve fuch a beautiful frame." Thefe
words naturally made me look at the
painting. I ftarted back, feized with
aftonifhment, when I beheld myfelf as if
in a mirror. I inftantly recollected to
have been perfuaded by young V******l,
after his accident, to let him have that
picture. Aftonifhment fettered my tongue;
and I fcarcely heard the Count fay,
"Faith, Marquis, you are grown much
handfomer, or the painter has not done
juftice to your face."

No fooner had the Count pronounced
thefe words, than a fide door opened, and
an old man, of a ftriking beauty, and an
elegant carriage, entered the apartment.
I bowed refpectfully, and was going to
thank

thank him for his kind invitation, when
he ran towards me, preffing me tenderly to
his bofom.

" I know you, Don Carlos," he added;
" and the difcovery you have made juft
now faves me a farther elucidation.  You
have preferved my fon's life; receive the
grateful effufions of a father's heart; but,
at the fame time, lament with me his untimely death."   With thefe words a torrent of tears gufhed down his cheeks.

" Gracious   Heaven!"   I   exclaimed,
kiffing the tears from his cheeks, " is it
poffible?"   A violent emotion, which had
been preparing all the morning, and only
had waited for a pretext of growing loud,
interrupted me here.  A copious ftream
of tears relieved my heart; I preffed him
to my bofom, and reclined my face on
his fhoulder.

" Yes, you are quite that fenfible, excellent man," he refumed, " whofe picture
my fon has fo frequently drawn to us with
enthufiaftic warmth.  Alas! his fate en-
vied

vied him the happinefs of feeing you once
more. He went into the army fome
years fince; a few months ago he was
thrown off his horfe, and died of the fall."
Here he paufed a few moments, and then
continued, "Yet you have loft nothing
by his death; the fon's friendfhip for you
has devolved to the father. I do not love
mankind; yet I wifh you would accept of
his place in my heart, and beftow, at
leaft, a part of your affection for my unhappy boy upon his father." It was very
natural that I replied I had loved him long
fince, and that I would endeavour to deferve his kind opinion. He now left me
reluctantly, turning to the Count. I told
him his name; and it fortunately happened that he was an intimate friend of
the Baron in his younger years. Our re-
verend hoft was rejoiced to renew an old
acquaintance, and we began foon to converfe fo cordially as if we had known one
another for years, and were members of
the fame family. . . .

Having

Having fpent about half an hour in the moft agreeable manner, the Baron faid to me, "I now will conduct you to my daughter, who has feen you already this morning, and inftantly recollected your features. You fee," he added, fmiling, "how ftrongly your image is imprinted on our hearts."

"Our affairs are in an excellent train!" the Count whifpered to me, while our kind hoft opened the door.

"Here, Adelheid, I bring you the friend of our Adolf!" the Baron faid, on our entering his daughter's apartment. "He has promifed me to be my fon and your brother."

The fweet girl fat upon the fofa, holding a book in her hand. She laid it down on our entrance, and rofe to meet us. She had exchanged her green hat with a ribbon of the fame colour, and her bofom was adorned with a white rofe. The reft of her drefs was nearly the fame as in the morning; her hair was in the fame charming

ing diforder, and a miniature picture depended from her swelling bofom.   It was
a manly face; but fortunately I thought
that it was the picture of her brother.

An amiable confufion blufhed on her
beautiful countenance.   My fecret agitation did, indeed, render me very unfit for
clofe obfervation: yet I perceived in her
timid looks, and on the faint blufhes of
her dimpled cheeks, certain fymptoms
which gave nourifhment to my hopes.

An innocent girl is chiefly fwayed by
inftinct, when fhe meets the man whom
her artlefs heart has chofen without being
confcious of it.  The moft confummate art
could not have invented a more charming
reception than fimple nature effected here.
The vifible tremour which glided through
her frame was a filent confeffion that
fomething more than the requeft of her
father prompted her to do what fhe did
afterwards.   Her heart fpoke through her
looks, though it was afraid of being underftood.  The image, and, if I do not
flatter

flatter myfelf too much, the beautified image, of her fecret dreams was led into her arms by her own father, to cherifh it as a brother. But who can force the human heart not to overftep the limits prefcribed by parental authority?

The father did not underftand his daughter completely.. He imagined that fhe did not anfwer his wifhes, and his tendernefs for me, as much as he had expected. "How!" faid he, "does Adelheid thus coldly receive the friends of her father, and her fecond brother?" Her looks could, however, have made him fenfible of his miftake; they intreated for indulgence, and at the fame time made the fweeteft confeffion. He fmiled benevolently at her confufion; and encircling his daughter with his arm, preffed her to my bofom, requefting me to embrace my fifter. Her cheeks burned, and my lips quivered. This was all that I was able to obferve.

I now

I now led her to her fofa, prefenting
the Count to her; and fhe returned his
courtly civility in a manner which betrayed the moft accomplifhed education.
I now was more at leifure to make obfervations, and my eager foul was abforpt in
the contemplation of her exquifite charms.
I had travelled much, and feen a great
many beautiful women; I even had poffeffed a wife adorned with heavenly
charms; and my imagination added to
her image, which was deeply engraven in
my foul, perfections which the original,
perhaps, never had; but here my boldeft
dreams were more than realized; I frequently doubted that I was awake.

Her foul, which foon recovered its
wonted flight, to unfold all its perfections, enchanted me irrefiftibly by
its romantic turn. I never fhould have
thought it poffible that fuch pure and juft
notions of human life could be treafured
up in that beautiful mind, which evidently
had received rather a fingular turn. Even
the prejudices of education, the national
notions

notions of her country, and the frailties
of the human heart, had, either by accident, or by an innate talent, given birth
to adorable virtues. What an angelic
heart was here to gain!

A walk in the garden being propofed,
fhe took hold of my arm with the innocent familiarity of a fifter; ftopped at her
favourite fpots, and informed me, with
an inchanting fimplicity, where fhe fometimes had thought of me. "Don't be
angry, dear Marquis," fhe added, "if I
now and then, perhaps, have intruded
upon your dreams by an obfcure omen;
for I really believe that this is poffible;
and Adolf repeated your name conftantly
towards the end of his life."

How fwiftly did the hours elapfe in the
company of that angel! The Count,
who was elated with joy at my happinefs,
completely accommodated himfelf to the
nature of her ideas, and in a fhort time
fpoke in the fame enthufiaftic ftrain that
was fo peculiar to her. Adelheid found
him

him very amiable, and told it him without referve. I was feveral times in danger of giving way to jealoufy; yet fhe always re-conciled me again by the tendernefs fhe evinced for me, and by numberlefs little endearments. The father took an artlefs and cordial fhare in the innocent flow of our fpirits. The firft rapture of joy was, however, of no long duration.

## CHAPTER IX.

THE Baron had made us promife, the firft evening after our our arrival, to ftay fome weeks with him; and thefe weeks were gradually extended to months. Adelheid's natural ferioufnefs returned by degrees. The Baron was fond of hunting, notwithftanding his age and infirmity; it being likewife the favourite diverfion of the Count, they were almoft the whole day in the foreft; and I was fond of no-thing. A fmall, well felected library did, indeed, agreeably fill up many of my hours;

hours; yet ftill many dreadful chafms were left, and I was obliged to have recourfe to walking to fhake off the heavinefs of time.

Adelheid being fond of exercife, we frequently met in the gardeh, where we were leaft difturbed. She feemed to have dedicated the morning fo religioufly to ferious occupations, that I would have intruded upon her on no account. I was, befides, in a very anxious fituation. I was fenfible of her attachment to me; but could I venture to prefume that this was any thing elfe than a fifter's love?

As for myfelf, I loved her with an unfpeakable ardour, with an uncommon patience, and an unexampled refignation. I was formerly too proud to receive laws from the female fex, but now faw myfelf at once reduced to the moft obedient fubmiffion. A young girl directed the courfe of my thoughts at pleafure, and guided the current of my ideas. I had completely loft the dominion over myfelf, was

4                              unexpectedly

unexpectedly deprived of what formerly conftituted my greateft pride, and there were hours when I fhed tears at that lofs.

The name of a fifter entitled her to many innocent familiarities which tranf-ported me beyond myfelf. The language of friendfhip flowed from her lips, and I was fure her heart did not give them the lie; yet fhe never difplayed one of thofe finer fymptoms of a ftrong, over-power-ing paffion; appeared to apprehend and to divine nothing; was always of the fame temper, without either referve or caprice. I did not know that there are female hearts of a nature different from that of the generality. What Adelheid had in common with the reft of her fex, with refpect to love, I miftook for a pe-culiarity of all paffions, and tormented myfelf with my own feelings at a time when I could have been completely happy.

We generally took a walk when the day began to decline. She took familiarly hold of my arm when we were alone; we rambled

rambled through different parts of the garden, and a large feat of turf, in the moſt diſtant corner, was commonly the ſpot to which we reſorted at laſt. Adelheid always grew more ſerious, and at length even melancholy, when we approached it, and I was taken with the ſame mood. The compaſs of this world was too narrow for her ſoul; ſhe gathered matter for new images in other regions: night ſtole upon us, and threw a deeper gloom over our dreams. A ſweet melancholy frequently made us weep, without our being able to account for it. I was generally ſo much agitated, that the power of utterance failed me. She then reclined upon my ſhoulder, and looked at me with eyes full of benign tenderneſs. One evening, when we were in the ſame melancholy diſpoſition, ſhe took hold of my hand, and preſſing it with affection, ſaid, "Dear Carlos, the diſpoſition of your fiſter renders her very unhappy: it would be very well if ſhe were not to ſojourn much longer in this world. But

VOL. III.        L        would

·would you then continue to remember me; and do you think you will know me again in another world?"

This and fimilar fcenes overwhelmed me with a fpeechlefs melancholy, which gradually began to prey on my vitals. She perceived it, and caught the contagion. The Baron, too, was grieved at my alarming fituation. The Count afked me, with tender fympathy, what ailed me? But what could I reply? He imagined that I was happy.

We met one evening in the garden, equally immerfed in that gloomy melancholy. I had been in a violent agony of mind all the day long, and almoft diftracted. Being impatient to get rid of that defponding mood, I took up my gun, and went into the park, where l wandered about till evening was already far advanced. No one knew where I was; and when I was returning to the caftle, I met fome fervants, who had been fent in fearch of me. Having fent them back, I climbed over the wall of the park, to come

to

to the caftle by a fhorter way, and, to confefs the truth, to meet Adelheid, who generally took a walk at that time.

I really met her, after a fhort ramble through the garden, abforpt in profound reverie, and walking with trembling fteps. She did not obferve me, although I was only a few paces diftant from her, being occupied with a rofe, which fhe alternately took from her bofom and replaced again. She was pale and dejected, carrying my cane in her hand, upon which fhe reclined, and frequently fixed her looks. I faw her ftart feveral times, looking around with a ghaftly afpect, and moving her hand as if fpeaking with fome perfon. At length fhe faw me ftanding clofe by her fide, began to ftagger, and I had fcarcely time enough to receive her in my arms.

"Good God! Marquis, where have you been?" fhe faid, collecting herfelf immediately; but that very moment a new misfortune happened. My gun being fufpended round my fhoulder by a ftrap, I pufhed it back to be better able to fup-

port

port Adelheid; but it was unhappily
cocked; the trigger came againſt the
branch of a ſmall tree, the fuſil went off,
and the ball wounded one of my fingers.
It bled copiouſly; and my hand being
lifted up, the blood ſtreamed into the face
and on the boſom of the Baroneſs.

This accident reſtored her entirely to
the full uſe of her ſenſes, inſtead of de-
priving her of it.  "Eternal God! what
have you done?" ſhe exclaimed, terrified,
and inſtantly pulled me towards an adjacent arbour, to examine my wound,
poured the contents of her ſmelling bottle
upon her handkerchief, and tied it carefully
up.  Having dreſſed my wound with
anxious alacrity, ſhe aſked me tenderly,
"Do you ſuffer great pains, dear Marquis?"
"Very little on my hand," I replied.
"Good God! are you wounded in another
place beſides?"  "Alas! here, here I have
violent pains!" pointing at my heart.
"What pains you there? Will you not tell
it your fiſter?" ſhe reſumed, taking hold
of my hand.  "Deareſt Adelheid, how
can

can I deferve that angelic goodnefs, how
can I make amends for your uncommon
tendernefs?" "Is this all that pains you?
Have you not deferved my love long fince?
The beft amends you can make for my
tendernefs is to return my love."

"O, then, I have deferved it, and
made ample amends; and you, Adelheid,
are in *my* debt. After this poor heart of
mine has wafted almoft all its vital powers
in a namelefs grief, you afk why it bleeds?
Oh! it is dreadful to love without hope;
and a *tranquil* return of a *violent* paffion is
more galling to a fpoiled, infatiable heart,
than the moft rancorous hatred."

A torrent of tears gufhed from her eyes,
and fhe began, after a fhort paufe, "You
are very unhappy, Carlos, if my tendernefs
does not fuffice you. I have frequently
afked myfelf, in the hours of filent melancholy, whether I am capable of a more ardent love than that which my heart feels for
you? I do not think I am. Tell me, dear
Carlos, what do you defire me to do?"
"What I defire? Can words defcribe

L 3                     that?

that? I wifh that Adelheid would live only for her Carlos, who knows no other happinefs but that of thinking of his fweet fifter, and would fhed his laft drop of blood to purchafe her felicity."

" Is that all my Carlos wifhes? Is not your image the fweeteft and the only ob- ject of my dreams and of my happieft hours? Does not every bleffing of my life depend upon your affection? Does not my heart beat ftronger, and my counte- nance affume a deeper hue, when I fee you? Does not your image follow me every where like my fhadow? Are you not the only object of my pride, and the fole arbiter of my happinefs? Shall I quit, for your fake, father, family, and friends; or live with you in a dreary folitude upon roots? Speak only, Carlos, and your Adel- heid will cheerfully obey. The world, nay eternity itfelf, would be a lonely de- fert to me without you!"

" Then you confent to become my wife; my faithful, ever adored wife?"

" Wife,

"Wife, or fifter. Is there any difference? Or do you think I have a ftronger claim to your love as wife? Here is my hand; I will be any thing you wifh me to be."

On our return to the caftle, we met the Baron, and the Count, who alfo had gone in queft of me, and with rapture embraced the recovered fon and friend. I was happier than words can defcribe, but found it impoffible to join in the lively fallies of their fportive humour. Adelheid was in the fame predicament. The Baron perceived our mutual tranfport, and his cheerfulnefs encreafed.

I went, on the fubfequent morning, to the Baron, as foon as he got up, and dif-covered the whole to him. He conducted me filently to his daughter, who, as well as myfelf, encircled his knees, and, lift-ing us up with tears of affection in his eyes, faid kindly, " God blefs you, my children: you have prevented me." S******i almoft was frantic with joy. Be-fore a month elapfed Adelheid was my wife.

We

We refolved to fpend the fummer in the country, and to go to Paris the enfu ing winter. We were unanimous in all our refolutions. The Count was looked upon as a member of our family, and had rendered himfelf as neceffary to the Baron and Adelheid as he was to myfelf. How unfpeakably charming was the fummer to me! I never had enjoyed the fine feafon with fo much hilarity and unclouded contentment. We became every day more fufceptible of the bleffings of a domefticated life; and our fociable happinefs affumed a livelier complexion, and encreafed with every hour. I generally fpent the morning in private with my wife; the dinner bell fummoned us to more common pleafures. Every one of us regaled our fociable circle, after dinner, with the new ideas and obfervations he had gathered in the courfe of his activity in the houfe and abroad.

Adelheid was of a very ferious character, and my joviality was gradually mellowed by her turn of thinking. She foon
desired

defired me to relate my hiftory, and loved
to hear me fpeak of Elmira. She was
pleafed with her melancholy difpofition,
and lamented her misfortunes; but conceived more predilection for the fpirit of
the confederation, in which they origi-
nated, than I wifhed: fhe found its principles good, and cenfured me now and
then for having acted with too much
impetuofity of paffion. We difcourfed
on this fubject every evening which found
us alone. While fhe attempted to penetrate deeper into the character of the different circumftances, fhe did, indeed, not
reconcile me to a fociety that had caufed
me fo many fufferings, but, neverthelefs,
fubdued my averfion from its principles.

The choice of our fociable pleafures
depended on our humour and on circumftances. Adelheid hunted, fifhed, or
walked, with us in the park. She fang
uncommonly well, and played the piano-
forte to perfection. I played the flute to-
lerably well: the Count was an adept on
feveral inftruments, and the old Baron
was

was delighted with our little concerts. Reading, and the mutual relation of our adventures, filled up the hours which were not dedicated to thefe and to more ferious occupations. None of us had ever enjoyed fo much unclouded happinefs for fo long a period, and none of our fociable circle had ever been fo completely fenfible of his felicity.

Thus autumn ftole upon us unawares. We poftponed our departure from time to time, till we could delay it no longer, if we wifhed to go to the capital. Having informed Count S****** of my marriage, he wrote almoft every poft day, urging me to come as foon as poffible to Paris. We departed, at laft; and at the latter end of November arrived at the capital. The political fituation of France was, at that time, not yet arrived at that critical ftate, as to caufe a great alteration in the fociable circles. I found my old friends again, united by the bonds of intimacy, and was welcomed with cordial joy. The Count appeared to be cheerful; and, although

not

not completely happy, yet fatisfied with his Caroline.

It may be eafily conceived what a noife the appearance of my wife made at Paris, where every new face charms and attracts the general notice of the fashionable circles. She eafily found out the proper fociable tone which fuited every circle to which fhe was introduced; became foon the favourite of all affemblies, and the idol of her acquaintances. She grew in a fhort time very intimate with Caroline, notwithftanding the difparity of their characters. The Baron was animated with new vigour, joined in all our diverfions, and forgot the imbecillities of his advanced age. S******i was his conftant attendant and companion; and Don Bernhard was an agreeable addition to our domeftic circle. We all were happy, or at leaft, appeared to be fo, when a new accident feemed to be going to difturb our pleafure. Count S****** became, foon after our arrival at Paris, a riddle to myfelf and all his acquaintances. He grew fad, dif-

fatisfied,

fatisfied, abfent, and irafcible. His whims were foon very troublefome to us, and he frequently treated his lady in a very harfh manner. I perceived that he preferred Adelheid's company to all other fociety; but without concluding therefrom upon the real caufe of his extraordinary change, looked upon it as the effect of the fimilarity of their characters, and as an encouragement of his melancholy. I cemented, therefore, that friendfhip as much as poffible, inftead of throwing the leaft impediment into his way. Adelheid, confiding in me and my knowledge of the Count's character, made no difficulty to admit his vifits without reftraint, and to receive from him an attention which fhe confidered as a matter of courfe in a friend of her hufband. I do not know what particular information S******i had received of the fecret caufe of his behaviour: in fhort, he, as well as Don Bernhard, grew every day colder to him, and jointly endeavoured to interrupt his intimacy with my wife, by throwing many little impediments into his way.

way. This ferved, however, only to add fuel to the flame: he intruded himfelf every where upon her; and at length pro-voked the voice of flander to fuch a de-gree, by the violence of his paffion, that S******i and Don Bernhard thought it their duty to inform me of it in plain . terms. I did, indeed, ridicule them for their fufpicion, but refolved to keep a watchful eye over him, and to take the firft opportunity to fpeak to Adelheid about it.

This opportunity offered itfelf fooner than I imagined; for fhe came one evening, after my return from company, to my apartment, holding a paper in her hand, and fhedding a torrent of tears.

" Deareft Adelheid!" I exclaimed, " what is the matter?" Having fent my valet away, fhe fat down by my fide, and began, with a trembling voice, " Carlos, I cannot conceal the infult I have received any longer from you. It would be crimi-nal in me to fpare your friend on the pre-fent occafion. You certainly have ob-ferved how Count S****** has behaved to

me

me for some time.   Read this note, which
I have found this moment on my dressing
table."   She gave me the note and I read:

   "Don't  fear,  beautiful  Marchionefs,
" that I shall  betray the secret  your eyes
" have confessed to me.   Will you receive
" to-morrow  night, at eight o'clock, be-
" neath the  large lime-tree, a vow which
" my looks have made  to you some time
" since?——Lewis, Count of S******."

It  was  the  Count's  hand  writing; I
could not be mistaken.   My indignation
was, at first, so vehement, that I flung it
rather  violently  upon  the  table,  and
knocked  a glass down.   The servant,
whom I had sent out of the room, returned,  asking  if I  had  rung  for  him?
Having ordered him to retire, I embraced
my wife, and promised to remove that little interruption of her tranquillity, without having recourse to violent measures. I
only begged  her  not to change her deportment to the Count, and to leave every
thing to me.

                                    She

. She seemed, indeed, to leave me with great tranquillity, but was actually far from being easy, and could not help informing her father of it. The Baron could conceal nothing from S******i, and the latter communicated it to Don Bernhard. They all agreed that I ought to meet the Count in the room of my wife, and the latter promised to be present on that occasion.

I was of the same opinion, and resolved to adopt their advice. The Count was, during the day, rather easier than usual. I repaired to the great lime-tree before it had struck eight o'clock, and was astonished to find S****** already there. He read a paper, and kissed it repeatedly; but no sooner did he see me, than he exclaimed, with the greatest fury, " Hell and damnation! I am betrayed: but you, monster in human shape, shall not escape me a second time." With these words he rushed upon me sword in hand.

I was not unarmed, and defended myself against his furious attack; taking all possible care that he should not run against

5

the

the point of my fword. I exclaimed un-
interruptedly, " For God's fake, Lewis,
defift, and hearken to me!" But all my
entreaties were fruitlefs. He uttered.
dreadful curfes, foaming and grinding his
teeth. I difarmed him, at length, and
flung his fword into the adjacent thicket.
He looked up to heaven, and ejaculated
the moft fhocking execrations.

Loud cries behind me now attracted
my attention. I looked round, and difcerned Bernhard's red coat through the
gloom of night. He was wreftling with
a white figure, and on the point of fink-
ing to the ground. Now he actually dropt
down. I haftened, half frantic, to affift
him: a dagger glittered over his head in
one hand of his antagonift, while the
other endeavoured to ftop his mouth with
a handkerchief. I pierced his opponent
in the firft violence of my paffion, and
in that moment perceived that he was
*Amanuel.* Tearing the bandage from his
head, I beheld *Alfonfo*, my faithful fervant, at my feet.

END OF THE THIRD VOLUME.

Lightning Source UK Ltd.
Milton Keynes UK
UKHW020016100223
416721UK00002B/432

9 781015 695641